# FIGHTING FOR MR. BEAUTIFUL

## ETERNAL CITY LOVE, BOOK 2

### CATERINA PASSARELLI

ISBN-13: 9780692556023
ISBN-10: 0692556028

Covered designed by Najla Qambers Designs

For more, visit www.CaterinaPassarelliBooks.com

## 1

**Leo**

"Call the police!" I shout into the mob of gawkers surrounding me. "Call the police!"

Elena's lacy white top soaks through in blood.

Her blood.

I'm holding onto her for dear life on the ground amongst a sea of onlookers.

My mind races. I can't focus on anything except for this beautiful woman in my arms ... suffering in pain.

First responders get to us in minutes. Elena is lifted into the back of the ambulance looking small and frail. I jump into the back of the vehicle with her. I will never let her out of my sight, even for a second.

After whispering her love for me, she went unconscious, and I can't get her to respond or wake up.

"She's been shot!" I shout to anyone who will listen. "She won't wake up!"

The paramedic looks at me, and I know he recognizes my face. Everyone has the same wide-eyed expression when they do.

"*Signor* Forte, we will do all we can." He cuts into Elena's romper where the bullet pierced her.

I think it's around her stomach, but I'm not doctor.

It hits me on the ride to the hospital that this woman, who just tried to break up with me, is the same woman who took a bullet to save my life.

How could she be so stupid yet so brave?

She should have let the bullet pierce me.

I deserve it.

Not her. Never her.

———

Seconds dragged to minutes which dragged to hours.

Hours have passed and yet no word on Elena's condition.

I was told she was going into surgery but that was the last I heard. All I can do is pace the waiting room like a maniac. I haven't been given any updates. I'm either going to throw up or break everything in this damn building.

She wanted us to be an official relationship for so long, and I fought her at every turn.

I wanted her to see that I am not the right person for relationships or marriage—it's just not what I know.

I'm a billionaire CEO and an Italian one at that. Love isn't supposed to be in my cards. Women only want me for my money or for a great fuck—which before Elena I was perfectly happy to provide.

That was until the moment she took my breath away in the coffee shop the day I met her. She turned everything in my life upside down with her smart mouth, delicious body, and big heart. She's pushed me to see I can love someone, but she has no clue this effect she's had on me.

In fact, she tried breaking up right before the shooting happened, talking about how she's not good enough for me—that's fucking crazy!

I need to tell her how I feel; she deserves that much. I am the one not good enough for her—it's not the other way around.

Pace, pace, pace—I can't stop pacing. I'm going to wear a hole through this ugly, sterile, white hospital floor. The last time I was in a hospital waiting room was when my Papá passed away. I can't bare it. It smells like bleach and hand sanitizer, masking death and desperation. Fear pours out of the walls from each sick person and their family members.

I'm on edge and I hate this feeling. I need to be in control; I'm always in control.

When the ambulance brought us here the hospital staff tried to shut me out because I am not Elena's family, but this one time I'm happy I can pull a few strings. My family has donated more to this hospital than anyone else.

I am not leaving Elena's side. Family or not.

*Bella, you have to pull through this. God, you stubborn woman, you can't leave me!*

Continuing to pace like a madman, a group of Americans push past me to rush the front desk speaking English loudly.

Everyone in the room looks over at the commotion. They ask about Elena's condition. Their faces display a mixture of shock and tears, and they're begging for answers—this must be what I look like too. I'm reflected in their faces, her true family.

"Excuse me, are you here for Elena Scott?" I ask.

Five faces turn to look at me.

"Holy shit! Leonardo Forte in the flesh." A loud blonde shouts. Her jaw drops and her eyes go wide. "What's going on with Elena? We booked the first flight out of Michigan when we heard the news. Tell us something, anything!"

We'll get to introductions later I guess; I know her family must be dying for any information. I would be too.

"Elena was pierced by a bullet in the spleen. She's in surgery right now. That's all I've been told." Looking at their panicked faces, I wish I had more to share.

"Who shot her?" the woman I'm assuming is Elena's mother whispers. She looks like she's seen a ghost.

"The police are still looking for the person responsible. We were in a crowded area on a public street when the shooting took place. It came out of nowhere. Witnesses are saying different things. I think the only person who actually got a good look at the shooter was Elena."

"Why would someone shoot her? This doesn't make any sense. Elena doesn't have any enemies," says a tall man with salt and pepper hair, who I guess is her father.

Under any other circumstances, I would feel nervous to meet the father for the first time, but right now we all feel the same thing: anxiety.

"The shooter wasn't aiming for Elena. Their aim was on me, but Elena jumped in front of me. She saved my life." I can't meet their eyes, and I can't accept the fact myself.

She put herself in harm's way for me. She could die because of me. No one has ever done anything as selfless for me before, ever.

"Fuck. No way? Man, she's got it bad for you Leo," the blonde says.

*Who the hell is this girl?*

We walk toward the sitting area and gather around each other for support.

"I'm Rebecca, Elena's mom," says the middle-aged woman with medium length brown hair—the same color as her daughter's—as she puts out her hand.

After what I just told them, I'm surprised they still want to talk to me. It's my fault their daughter is in this hospital and the reason they are distressed. But I grab her hand quickly before she has a chance to change her mind.

"Leonardo," I say, shaking hands with her father, Steven, her sister, Christina, and her brother, Ian. The crazy blonde turns out to be her best friend, Sophie. With the formal introductions out of the way, we sit down and play the waiting game.

A half an hour later, a doctor walks toward the waiting area and we all fall silent. *Please tell me my cara is okay.*

"*Signor* Forte." The doctor nods in the direction of Elena's family. "I take it you are her family?"

"Yes," Christina says on behalf of the silent group.

We all wait on the edge of our seats.

"I have good news. Elena is out of surgery. We were able to locate and remove the bullet, but we did have to perform an emergency surgery to remove her spleen. She lost a lot of blood. Currently she's unconscious. Her vital signs are good though because she is young and was in good physical condition, but we do not know when she will wake up."

Dizziness consumes my brain.

*Thank you, God!*

"Thank you, doctor!" Sophie rushes from her chair and embraces the doctor in a bear hug.

"A nurse will come out and let you know when it's okay to go back and see Elena," the doctor says before leaving us alone in the waiting room.

Rebecca and Steven hug each other and their kids. It's nice to see a family together.

In this moment, I wonder what it would be like if my father were still alive. I would guess my mom would be a hell of a lot different. Right now, she's cold as ice toward everyone, including Elena, except me.

Before I can ponder that idea, a nurse comes over and lets us know we can go back to Elena's room in the ICU in about ten minutes—two at time.

The nurse pulls me aside to let me know about my earlier request.

"*Signor* Forte, I know you want to take care of Elena's medical bills. I need you to fill out these forms." She hands me a clipboard full of papers.

"Sorry, not to intrude," Sophie chimes in. "But did I hear her say you were going to pay for Elena's medical bills?"

I don't want to make a big deal about this in front of her family or have the hospital ask them for any money. We should focus on Elena's health, not how the bills are going to get paid, especially when I can take care of them so easily.

I don't even know what kind of travel health insurance she has, if any.

"*Si*, it's no big deal." I wave her off as I fill out the forms so I can quickly hand them back to the nurse without drawing more attention.

"This is a very big deal," Sophie says, getting louder and attracting the attention of her whole family. "Elena is going to be pissed!"

*Pissed?*

"What the hell are you talking about?" I say, quickly realizing I'm too loud too.

Elena's family members stare at us.

*Remain calm Leo, you are in front of her family, even if her best friend is insane.*

"Elena does not take charity. Why would you have to pay anyway? Don't they have her insurance information?"

"She works in a *caffè*. I didn't even know she had insurance," I say.

Sophie busts out laughing. I'm definitely going to talk to Elena about her choice in friends. This one needs to go—she's no good for her.

"She works in a coffee shop? I didn't even know she knew how to turn on a coffee pot." Ian laughs too.

*What the hell is with these people? Maybe they are still in shock?*

"Elena hasn't told you yet, I'm guessing?" Sophie looks at me again with a smirk. "I told her she needed to, but I see the advice of her wise best friend means nothing to her."

Told me what?

Now I'm irritated. Everyone is part of some secret that I'm on the outskirts of.

"Elena doesn't need you to pay her medical bills. She's a millionaire … and she definitely has health insurance," Christina says.

"A millionaire? From selling shots of espresso? What are you talking about?" My mind races a hundred miles-per-hour.

Why is she working in a coffee shop?

How is she a millionaire?

And why didn't she tell me any of this?

And how stupid do I look right now?

"Elena owns Rock Star Media, the largest social media marketing firm in the United States. She came to Italy to relax after things were getting a little crazy back at home," Sophie says.

It's like someone has pulled a chair out from under me. Why wouldn't Elena tell me this? Does it matter to me? No, not at all. For richer or for poorer. *Fuck did I just think about wedding vows? What is going on with me?*

"I need a minute of fresh air." I walk toward the front doors of the hospital, but I'm quickly stopped by Mateo, my right-hand man.

"You don't want to go out there boss. The paparazzi have been camped out and they are waiting for anything. Vultures," he warns.

Mateo has worked for my family since I was a little kid. He used to be in the Italian army and then served on the police force. Now he's my bodyguard and driver, and for just about anything else I need help with, he's there. I trust his advice

*"Grazie Mateo."*

The press getting any more information about Elena is the least of my concerns. I wish they'd focus their attention on catching whoever did this.

## 2

***

**Elena**

My head pounds, surrounded by loud beeping sounds.

What did I do last night? Did I go out clubbing? I can't remember anything. Why is my stomach killing me? My throat is also on fire and it's incredibly dry.

*Alright Elena, open your eyes and face what you've gotten yourself into. This is the worst hangover in the history of hangovers*

*3 ... 2 ... 1.*

Eyes open. I'm in a hospital. Why am I in a hospital? The beeps come from big machines, and I've got IVs sticking out of everywhere. I'm alone in this room as well. Panic sets in.

*Wake up Elena, this is just a bad dream. A nightmare.*

Before I can press a red button attached to a cord in my bed, a young redhead nurse opens the door and walks into my room.

She looks shocked I'm awake. Surprise! *Get me out of here!*

The nurse calls for help. Is she speaking Italian? Okay this must really be some bizarre dream. Did I eat sushi last night? I have the strangest dreams after I eat sushi.

An entire team of nurses and a doctor now surround me. I hear talk of my vital signs, and charts are passed around.

My Italian may be a little rusty but I swear I hear the words spleen, consciousness, family, and shooter.

"Elena, how do you feel?" a man with a black bushy mustache asks.

Behind his glasses, he has gentle eyes.

As I start to speak, I feel as if a thousand needles stabbing my throat. "I could really use a glass of water."

The team looks shocked—like I've said something wrong—but a glass of water is suddenly placed in front of me. I chug the entire thing and look up as everyone stares, but no one says a word. I know they are waiting for me to speak again.

"Why am I in a hospital?"

Scanning their faces, I try to pick up on any clues as to the pain I'm in.

"Elena, you were shot in the spleen and had to have emergency surgery to remove it. You are okay, but it will take some time to heal. Probably weeks. You've been unconscious for three days."

*I was shot!*

"Shot ... me?" My mind races. "Are you serious? I don't understand. Who shot me?"

My vision tunnels and the room grows darker and darker before my eyes close again.

The last thing I hear before I pass out is a nurse shouting my name. They're pronouncing it wrong but that's when I remember they are Italians.

————

**Leo**

Elena woke up and then fell unconscious for two more days. It's been five days in this hellish hospital. When the doctors did get a chance to speak to her, they said she was disoriented, but they also said this is normal.

I've been living at this hospital, along with Elena's family and Sophie.

Work is on hold, my life is on hold, and I can't seem to function without knowing Elena is okay. More than okay—I want to hold her in my arms, take her home with me, kiss her, and tell her I love her.

We've been able to go back and sit in the room with her while we wait. I can't take it though, seeing her lying in that bed looking fragile and hearing the machines beeping. It all makes me crazy.

I want to pick her up and shake her awake.

I want to hear her tease me and call me that ridiculous nickname, Mr. Beautiful.

I want to smack her glorious round ass as she walks in front of me.

I want to laugh at all the crazy sarcastic shit she manages to come up with.

I want to take her out and watch other men's jaws drop when she turns their heads, but know that she's all mine.

I want to tell her that I'm over this 'friends' or 'lovers' bullshit—I want to be with her, forever.

I just want her to wake the fuck up.


**Elena**


I don't want to open my eyes because I know what I'll find: a hospital room. I remember just a few minutes ago that I opened my eyes and saw the doctor and nurses surrounding me. Apparently, I've been shot, which still baffles me.

I hear the loudest breathing and realize I'm not alone in this room.

It's time to face the person snoring next to my bed.

"Sophie," I say, spotting my best friend is asleep in the chair.

Her long blonde hair is tied in a wild bun and her clothes look like she's been sleeping in them for days. I know she's uncomfortable. I must have barely whispered her name because she doesn't move a muscle. "Sophie! Wake your ass up."

This time Soph jumps up out of the chair and nearly falls onto my bed.

"Elena, holy shit! I'm so glad you're awake," she says with tears streaming from her blue eyes. I don't think I've ever seen my tough-as-nails bestie cry before. Oh man, now she's going to make me cry.

"Oh no! Elena, why are you crying? Are you hurt?" Sophie looks at me like I'm a flimsy doll.

"No! Well, yes, but that's not why I'm crying. I'm crying because you're crying."Snot runs out of my nose.

Sophie busts out laughing and then I can't help but do the same. My gut hurts—I need to stop laughing! We're a mess of tears, snot, and laughter when the same redhead nurse walks into the room and stares at us like we are a bunch of damn fools.

"What, you've never seen anyone cry-laugh before?" Sophie says in her brass way.

The nurse leaves the room but is back in an instant with the same male doctor I saw earlier—his name badge reads 'Dr. Costa.'

"Elena, it's nice to see you laughing." He grabs a chart and jots down some information from the machine I'm hooked up to.

Sophie hands me a tissue and a glass of water—it's like she read my mind.

"Can someone please tell me what's going on? Earlier you told me I was shot?

"Earlier? Elena the last time we spoke was four days ago."

*Four days? I was out that long?*

"How long have I been in this hospital?"

"Nine days total, and we'd like to keep you here for a few more days of observation for your spleen."

I look toward my best friend and meet her blue eyes pleading for her to tell me, "How did this happen?"

Sophie looks at the doctor and he says, "You don't remember getting shot?"

Just as I'm about to answer, the most beautiful man I've ever seen — tall with thick dark hair and emerald eyes—walks in the room.

"Elena, *cara*, I am so happy you are awake!" The Italian model high-tails it to my bed.

"Do I know you?" I ask.

Everyone stares at me, Sophie's mouth hangs open, and it's eerie how quiet it gets.

I must have said the wrong thing.

"Elena, you don't recognize this man?" Dr. Costa says, the first to break the silence.

"No, should I?" I turn toward the hottie. "Are you a celebrity or something?"

"Oh my freakin' god!" Sophie says as the beautiful man stares at me with pleading eyes.

Studying his handsome face, I search hard for any clue of who he might be but ... nothing.

I would surely remember someone with a defined jawline like his.

"I'm really sorry. I have no clue who you are."

The tears fall again, but this time out of anxiety and sadness. I'm clearly missing something important right now.

"It's okay, Elena. Please don't cry," the man says in a deep voice with an Italian accent as he puts his hand toward mine.

Without thinking, I flinch and pull my hand back. I don't really do touchy-feely stuff with anyone—especially a stranger.

"Elena, what is the last thing you remember?" the doctor asks as I notice the redhead nurse is back in the room now.

I'm starting to hyperventilate with all of this attention.

"I remember going into the office to listen to Rock Star Media's presentation on how we should pick up romance authors as clients and test using Pinterest to sell their novels. I remember going to lunch with an investor, picking up my dry cleaning, and coming home to watch some random crappy documentary on Netflix with Zack."

No one says anything. I look from stone cold face to stone cold face.

"Wow," Sophie says.

"Sophie, is that not what happened?"

I turn toward the only person I know in this room and look into her scared eyes.

"Can I tell her?" Sophie asks the doctor.

"Tell me what? Would someone just spit it out? I can't take this bullshit anymore! I feel like I'm in some freak show with all of you staring at me with your mouths open." I notice my voice getting louder and louder. #Freakout

The man at my bedside laughs a deep rich laugh, and I can't help but stare at him. "Oh you think that's funny?" I say toward Mr. ... I don't even know his name.

"I've been waiting nine days for you to wake up and hear your sassy mouth," he says.

He's been waiting for me? My sassy mouth?

"Elena, you are in a hospital in Rome. You took a little vacation from Rock Star Media and you've been living here for months. You are dating Leonardo," Sophie says as she nods toward the man who can't stop staring at me.

*Wait ... did she say dating Leonardo?*

Now it's my turn to laugh! I can't help it. I laugh so hard that I grab my belly. Ouch! Flinching in pain, I feel a pull at my side.

"Elena, are you okay? Lay back and take it easy, *bella*," Leonardo says. He now sits on the bed next to me and holds my hand. I look at our hands together, not moving mine this time. I look up into his mesmerizing eyes—they look like stunning gems.

"I'm so sorry I don't remember you. I feel terrible."

I look back down at our hands, not being able to meet his eyes. I can't even imagine what it would be like to have someone I'm dating not remember me. I would be crushed. Leonardo seems to be holding it together—probably for me. I'm his girlfriend.

He takes his hand from mine and instead cups my chin, tilting my head up to meet his eyes.

"Elena, it's okay. You didn't do this on purpose. You saved my life." Now he looks down at the bed.

"How did I save your life?"

"That bullet wasn't aimed at you—it was aimed at me. You jumped in front of me, knocking us both to the ground. That's when I noticed you were bleeding."

His shoulders are slouched and his eyes are bloodshot.

I saved his life. I jumped in front of a bullet.

What the hell? The most daring thing I've ever done is play around with my stock investments. I wouldn't jump in front of a gun, unless it was for my family. Someone I loved. *Do I love him?*

"How long have we been dating?" I ask.

"We've known each other for a few months."

Why did he say 'known each other' not dating?

"I asked how long we've been *dating?*"

"That's complicated." Leonardo runs a hand through his thick hair. "We've recently become a couple but I met you right when you got to Italy."

I took a bullet for someone I recently started to date. This doesn't sound like me at all. What do I even know about this guy? My head hurts again from all the confusion and trying to remember.

"Do we love each other?"

I know it's a bold question to ask, but I need to know the situation between myself and this extremely handsome man, a man I normally wouldn't have the balls to talk to, let alone date.

"Yes. I love you Elena," Leonardo says with such strong conviction, looking me straight in the eyes.

His answer and his honesty thus far hit me deep in my feels. I can't help but put myself in his shoes and the tears well up in my eyes. Why can't I remember this man? I want to remember him so badly.

"I think Elena should take a little break. We still have some tests we want to run on her," says the doctor, coming to my rescue as the emotions overwhelm me.

When they leave me alone, I close my eyes and try to remember anything in Italy.

Nothing.

It's like turning on a television station but the screen is black.

I'm dating that man.

Really?

Sophie wouldn't lie.

He says we are in love.

Suddenly, I blush. Oh no. We've surely had to ... fuck. How could I forgot having sex with a hunk like that?

Not only am I irritated that I can't remember being shot but I also can't remember a man who looks like he'd rock my world.

# 3

## Leo

*Do I know you?*

Four words I never knew I couldn't bear to hear. How can she be my entire world and she doesn't have a clue who I am?

I feel a rush of emotions: anger, sadness, panic, and fear. What if she never gets her memories back?

Elena is mine, and I will help her do anything to remember us. She looked absolutely shocked that she would take a bullet for me. I don't know what feels worse: knowing she took a bullet that should have had me in a hospital bed or the fact that she doesn't remember it?

"Ah!" I scream as I knock over a hospital cart full of supplies, sending everything crashing to the floor.

"*Signor. Signor!*" the hospital security guard says as he runs at me when I sink to the floor and drop my head in my hands.

I will help her get her memories back or I will do everything in my power to give her even better ones. I will make sure she knows she is loved. I will fight to have Elena love me again, to look at me like she did before.

I vow this.

# 4

## Elena

Sophie comes back into my room and now that I have a minute alone with her I need all the dirty details.

"Your family must be in the lunch room so I snuck back in. I'll go back to the waiting room in a few minutes and get them. They are going to freak when they know you are awake. Wait ... you remember your family, right?"

I laugh at her terrible joke. "Wow! Sophie, I still remember that you are a bitch."

Leave it to Sophie to poke fun at someone who has a case of what the doctors are calling dissociative amnesia. They say it can be caused from a head injury or physical trauma and that my memories are repressed.

"I'm glad to see your memory loss didn't rob you of your sense of humor. Even if it comes at the cost of you calling me a bitch."

"Okay, so tell me the truth. What's the deal with this guy? Why did I grow a pair and take a bullet for him?"

"Girl, you've got it bad for him." She takes a seat next to my bed.

"Leonardo Forte is the most eligible bachelor in all of Italy and even though you were mad at him about that model, you fought hard for your relationship. Last I knew you were back together."

"What model?"

"Uhh, I shouldn't be talking about this stuff." She looks like a deer in headlights and that's rare for Sophie. "Leonardo should probably tell you."

"No." I hold my hand up. "As my best friend, *you* are going to tell me. I can't ask a guy I just met to explain something like that. What model? And how did I end up with Rome's most eligible bachelor?"

Questions swirl in my head, and before Sophie can give me any answers my mom, dad, brother, and sister burst through the door with a pair of nurses right behind them.

"There can only be two visitors in the room at a time," the nurses shout at my family.

My parents don't care, as they rush over to my bed and embrace me in hugs. I can't tell you how great it feels to have your family surrounding you. I look at all their faces and see the tears of joy in their eyes, and in that moment I am so happy and relieved that I remember each and every one of them.

These beautiful faces are my safe place.

"Elena, sweetheart, how are you feeling?" my mom asks.

Everyone has stayed in the room, and I bet on the other side of that door the nurses are fuming. But I'm glad my family is surrounding me.

"Physically, I'm sore. Mentally, I'm a mess."

"Because of the shooting?" Christina asks.

My sister has such a calming presence—always has. When I bossed her around, as the older sister should, she always kept a level head and went along with my crazy antics. Now she's a kindergarten teacher. I think I helped train her for that role nicely.

"Well, yes, because of the shooting but also because of the amnesia."

"Amnesia? What are you talking about?" my brother asks.

"The doctors say I have dissociative amnesia—I can't remember recent events. I have no memories at all of being in Italy, or of Leonardo."

My family members wide eyes do not hide the fact that they can't believe the news.

They ask more questions about my most recent memories, but luckily Sophie is here to fill them in.

I'm extremely tired, and I drift off to sleep, even with all the commotion around me.

———

I wake up to an empty hospital room. It's kind of eerie as I'm used to it being full of my loved ones. While tubes came out of me all over the place before, I'm only hooked up to one machine now, monitoring my heart rate.

I hope that's a sign that I'll be able to leave here soon. I want to go home.

*Wait, where's home for me?*

I can't believe I'm in Italy. Since I started Rock Star Media I haven't taken a single vacation. I've been 'go go go' since the day I signed my name on the dotted line and took out that business loan. Which, I'll have you know, my company paid back within its first year. I digress.

What drove me to leave my business behind for so long and pick up in another country? This sounds so unlike the conservative, sensible woman that I am. *That I used to be?*

The door gently swings open and the man from earlier, Leonardo, peaks his head inside. We lock eyes. Man, those emerald eyes are breathtaking. I'm jealous of the girl he remembers, who must have been able to stare into them whenever she wanted.

"I didn't know you were awake."

"I just woke up. Trying to collect my thoughts before facing my family again. And I hear the police are coming to get my statement soon. Everyone seems to have a lot of questions that I just can't answer."

Leonardo walks into the room and sits in the chair next to me. I notice he doesn't sit close to me on the bed like he did before. He's giving me my space, which I appreciate. I also notice that as he walks he carries himself with quiet confidence. Nothing boastful or cocky—it's extremely sexy.

I've been caught staring at him in silence and feel my cheeks tart to blush.

"How did we meet?" I ask, breaking the silence and my awkward staring.

"I came into the coffee shop you were working in—Stella's."

"I still can't believe I work in a coffee shop. Other than using my Keurig, I don't think I've ever made my own coffee before." I chuckle at my confession, my cheeks probably turning a whole new shade of red.

Did he like me because he thought I was domestic? I sure hope not.

"You weren't that good in the beginning, but Marco has taught you so much. You can make many different drinks and you even bake desserts." Behind his words I feel he has a sense of pride for me.

"Hold the phone! You're saying someone has allowed me into his precious kitchen to *bake* something and I haven't burned the place down to the ground yet? This blows my mind!"

Leonardo laughs and I can't help but stare at his gorgeous mouth and the sexiest, fullest lips I've ever seen. I don't know what's come over me, but I have the sudden urge to climb out of this hospital bed, crawl into his lap, and claim his mouth.

I suddenly realize that this is the first time we've been in the room alone together since the shooting. I also realize I've never had the urge to jump a man before. I'm not really a 'take charge' kind of woman when it comes to that kind of stuff.

And by 'stuff' I mean ... sex.

The machine tracking my heart rate shows the numbers are climbing—revealing how nervous, embarrassed, and horny I am just looking at Leonardo.

We both stare at the screen then fall into another awkward silence.

"I'm sorry that I don't remember you."

"I can't say that it doesn't break my heart that you now look into my eyes and see a total stranger. But, I also can't say that I'm upset as this was not your fault and you do not need to apologize for anything. I keep replaying in my head, over and over again, the moment you got shot. You are a crazy woman, but you are *my* crazy woman, and I can't believe you took a bullet for me. I will repay you and I will help you get your memories back."

No man has ever spoken to me like this before. The immature, cocky douchebags I dated before just wanted sex, a connection into the corporate world, or a sugar mama—I wasn't going to be any of those things, and most of those guys quickly dumped me.

"I don't want to let you down." I look down at my hands, which are balled into fists in my lap. I unclench them to release some stress.

Leonardo moves to the edge of his chair and leans in toward me. He cups my chin and lifts my face.

"Elena, you will never let me down. *Cara,* I love you. I know right now you don't love me, but I will fight to bring your memories back or make you fall in love with me all over again."

He speaks with such passion that he nearly brings me to tears. My eyes are watering when he hands me a tissue.

"You are unlike any man I have ever known. I don't give my heart away easily, I never have. I've always been guarded, especially around men, because my track record isn't stellar. But this," I say, waving my hands between us, "is something I want to fight for too."

I'm not sure of anything right now but this feels right.

## 5

It's been two days since leaving the hospital. I meet with the *Carabinieri*. "I don't remember a damn thing," was probably not what they wanted to hear from the only person who they believe saw the shooter.

Apparently I ran across the street toward Leonardo screaming and jumped in front of the bullet, which leads them to believe I saw danger.

But I don't even know the answer to the simplest question: was the shooter a man or a woman?

The news reports say there are no suspects or leads, and the police are asking anyone with information to come forward. Leonardo tells me that hundreds of people were around us on the street. He's desperately hoping people caught something on their smartphones.

Leonardo has offered a million dollar reward for anyone with information that leads to an arrest. The tip lines are now blowing up, but the police say most of it is bullshit.

It freaks me out that there's someone walking the streets who wanted to kill Leonardo. *Was I worried that my life was in danger before? Will the shooter try again?*

Even with a crazy shooter on the loose, I've decided to stay in Rome. I'm part of a story that's bigger than myself now. It's hard to explain, but I'm in no hurry to rush back to the life of an overworked, stressed CEO who never had any fun and dated a bunch of losers. I came here for a reason and I want to remember the things I've learned so far. I know my company is in good hands with Sophie's help, and I do get weekly reports.

Since I'm staying, Dr. Costa told me to go about my day as best as I could and the memories may flash back. He also said they may not. I have no clue what a 'typical day' was for me so I've had to rely on the people close to me here in Italy.

Yesterday I spent some time in Stella's Caffé hanging out with Marco, Alessandra, and Leonardo. I'm proud of my pre-amnesia self for getting out of my comfort zone and making new friends. Who was the last true friend I made before Sophie?

Marco treats me like I am his little sister, but I guess technically I am his boss. He tells me I saw he was in a desperate situation and I offered my help. I am the majority owner of Stella's Caffé. Go figure!

Alessandra? Damn this girl should be walking a runway! When she first saw me, she pulled me into the biggest hug with, of course, the Italian double-cheek kiss. She told me that we met in a gym and that I take her classes—I'm glad to see that I continued to value my fitness here in Rome. Just like Marco, I get a vibe that she's protective of me and wants to see me pull through.

Then there's Leonardo. Sweet Leonardo! He treats me like a queen, and I still can't remember anything about him. I'm constantly asking questions—I feel like Drew Barrymore in *Fifty First Dates*—as I get to know him all over again.

He's told me a lot, but I sense he's not telling the full story. Everything seems a little too happy-go-lucky—have we ever had a real fight? Knowing me, we definitely have, but he doesn't divulge any information when I ask uncomfortable questions.

I'll have to pull Alessandra or Sophie aside to get the scoop.

————

I spend the afternoon working my first shift at Stella's. The customers are so unbelievably kind. I can't remember the last time I went to work and left with a smile on my face—usually I'm pulling out my curly brown hair after everyone's demands. But not here!

I'm treated like I could be one of their family members. Everyone who comes to the register places their order and tells me a little story about how we met or what they know about me. #Loved

"They really love you here," Marco says to me during a mid-afternoon lull.

"You know it's kind of silly but I'm glad my memory is gone in moments like these. Hearing them say such touching things, it fills me up with joy," I confess as I wipe down the espresso machine.

We get back to work when I hear the *click, click, click* of a pair of high heels and my eyes perk up. I haven't forgotten my fashion sense—it sounds like Valentino.

I turn away from the machine toward the granite counter and see a tall woman with long brown hair striding toward me. She's wearing an extremely short dark blue Gucci dress, and she hasn't cracked a smile yet. She definitely looks out of place in this caffé.

"*Ciao*, welcome to Stella's," I say, mustering my fakest customer service smile. She drops her blue Chanel clutch on the counter a little too violently and looks up at me with iced cold brown eyes.

"*Buongiorno*, Elena," she says in the highest pitched voice I've ever heard. Nails on a chalkboard kind of voice.

*She knows me?* This woman acts nothing like the others I've met so far. If we're friends, then I'm embarrassed that I just welcomed her to the caffé like a complete stranger. Oh well, let's blame it on the amnesia.

"I'm sorry, I don't remember your name."

"Elena dearie, I'm Victoria, *your friend*. I heard about your little memory issue," she says, waving her hand around her own head, "And wanted to stop by to see how you were doing."

Little memory issue? Did she put a strong emphasis on the word 'friend'? This woman does not seem nice—why are we friends?

"*Grazie* for coming to check on me. Could you help me try to remember you? How did we meet?"

"Through my ex-boyfriend ... Leonardo."

Why am I dating one of my friend's ex-boyfriends? I think that's

24

against some kind of girl code. I have never been a home wrecker before. If I can't get my own man, then I don't want someone else's.

"I'm sorry. You dated Leonardo? When did you break up?"

The woman huffs, sounding bored with this conversation, and she picks at her long fingernails, avoiding eye contact with me.

"Elena, I'm sorry I don't have time to go into all these details. I'm late for a luncheon. Get me an iced espresso with a dash of water."

Damn, she's bossy to her friends.

I work on her drink, but my mind can't stop wondering about who exactly this woman really is. Did I end her relationship with Leonardo? She's okay with me dating him and us being friends? Why haven't any of my other friends mentioned her?

"Have you met Aurora yet?" Victoria says, as I ring up her order and she hands me her credit card.

"Aurora? Is she one of our friends too?"

"Well, now that I think about it, you don't really like her. You caught Aurora and Leonardo making out at his birthday party, a party he brought you to, but you know she may still be hanging around." She quickly downs her shot, leaving the empty cup on the counter, completely ignoring the fact that she's just dropped a bomb, and adds, "I can't stand around and chit-chat all day. Some of us have hard work to do. *Ciao ciao.*"

And just like she *click, click, clicked* those Valentino heels into the coffee shop, she turns around and clicks away in a big hurry.

What the fuck just happened? I'm surely not in Michigan anymore.

———

Leonardo and I have dinner plans tonight that I should get ready for, but I just can't stop thinking about what that Victoria chick said. Leonardo cheated on me? But I clearly took him back, right? Fuck this amnesia! I want my memories back right this second.

Before my pity party can go on any longer, there's a loud knock at the door. Time to get your answers, Elena! Don't let him skate around your questions. This is the kind of pep talk I need because, outside of a boardroom, I'm not good with confrontation.

I open the apartment door and Leonardo stands there looking devastatingly handsome in a button-up dark purple dress shirt and dark black jeans with black dress shoes. He looks relaxed yet refined at the same time. His emerald eyes shine and light up his olive skin. Man, why does one guy have to look so sexy?

*Snap out of it!*

"*Ciao* handsome!" I immediately regret flirting.

I remind myself I'm on a mission to get to the bottom of our relationship. Bottom ... yeah that's where I'd like to be. Oh my god, play a little hard to get woman! #Mortified #Horny

"*Ciao bella*, you look stunning." Leonardo puts his hand on my lower back and escorts me out of the apartment.

We meet his driver, Mateo, at the bottom of the stairs on the small street outside and step into his black luxury town car. The car soon smoothly drives away.

"Did you have a good day at work?" I ask. Is this the kind of stuff we talk about?

"It was non-stop meetings all morning, and then we had to host team members from around the country in our office to work on a project we are about to launch," he replies as he scoots himself closer to me.

I can smell his cologne—leather, woodsy, and pure man.

"Meetings are the worst! I established a 15-minute 'quick meeting' rule at our company so that everyone can get in and get out with the best ideas without having to sit around and make small talk about bullshit," I blab.

Not saying a word, Leonardo looks at me with his mouth hanging open like I have three heads.

"What's wrong? Do I have something in my teeth?" I say while I hurry to reach for a compact in my clutch.

Please don't tell me I've got a piece of lemon pepper shrimp scampi from lunch stuck in my teeth! My luck would be to go on a date with a completely gorgeous stud and have spinach in my teeth.

"No your teeth are *perfecto*. I'm sorry, I'm not used to hearing you talk about your work. I like hearing your ideas, you are very smart, and it's a turn on. I hope you can share more ideas with me about your company's policies."

"Wait, what?" I turn toward him. "We are dating and I never talked about my work? I eat, sleep, and breathe my work. This doesn't sound like me at all."

If I didn't win him over as a fellow CEO, then what the hell did we talk about?

He looks into my eyes intensely.

"I did not know what you did back in America until after the shooting when your sister told me in the hospital. I felt a little foolish finding out that way. I knew your work had something to do with social media, but that's all you'd ever say. You never really told me just how successful you were. You seemed to avoid the topic when I'd bring it up, and I didn't want to press you."

I look out the window at the old buildings passing by and then back at Leonardo.

"I wonder why I didn't say anything?" Looking up at him, we both have puzzled looks on our faces. "Maybe I was trying to get away from the string of terrible boyfriends I had in America. I dated guys that only wanted me for my money or to connect them with someone they thought would make them successful too."

My confession embarrasses me. I'm really making myself seem like a catch.

"*Bella,* I don't know why you didn't open up about your past life with me, but I do know that none of those things matters to me. You can work in a caffé for the rest of your life and I will love you. You can run a social media empire and I will feel the same. Your personality, your heart, your beauty, and even your sarcastic wit drew me into you."

Be still my heart.

This guy makes me feel like I'm a rock star. How does he find just the right words to say to touch my heart?

The car stops and we're outside a restaurant that looks like it's in the countryside. Twinkling ropes of outdoor lights make the patio look romantic, and I have this feeling in my stomach that I've been here before.

"Leonardo, have we been here before?" I ask as I climb out of the door Mateo opens for me.

"*Si,* this restaurant belongs to a family friend of mine and I brought you here to meet him. Do you remember anything about your visit?"

Leonardo's emerald eyes study my face. I know he's hoping memories are flooding back in this moment.

"Sadly, no. I don't remember being here before. I just had a *feeling* like I knew this place. It's hard to explain," I say, feeling a little defeated and hoping I don't sound crazy.

"That's okay. Let's go enjoy our date. We can make new memories here."

Dinner is lovely—great food and great company. I can see why I made it a point to hit the gym—the food in Italy is ridiculously amazing and I could easily gain a good 30 pounds if I wasn't careful.

Tonight we started with a small serving of bacon and scallops potato gnocchi, followed by arugula and roasted fruit salad with panettone croutons, and then our main course of fettuccine Alfredo. And let's not forgot about the endless bread dipped in olive oil!

Oh. My. God. To freakin' die for. #CarbsOverload

I meet *Zio* Armando and his granddaughter, Abrianna, for what I'm told is the second time. They both embrace me into tight squeezes and double-cheek kisses. I'm glad to add them to the collection of friends I've made so far.

Speaking of friends, I don't know how to bring up the subject of my very questionable friend and the gossip she dropped on me at work this morning. But there's no better time than the present.

"Leonardo, who is Aurora?" I whisper because I can't believe I'm throwing this topic out there so ballsy. Do we talk about intimate things? We didn't even talk about what I did for a living.

"Elena, where is this question coming from? Who told you about Aurora?" Leonardo puts his napkin on the table. *So he's not denying her existence* Maybe he really did cheat on me. *Not again with another cheater!*

"Does it really matter who told me? That doesn't change the fact that I asked you about her. I'd like you to answer me, please."

He hasn't even answered yet, and I feel myself shrinking back into my old defensive shell. I shut down completely when I'm being treated like I'm worthless.

"*Cara,* Aurora was a woman I went on dates with before I knew you."

"What about at your birthday party?" I fire the question out at rapid speed, trying not to lose my strength.

He wipes his eyes with his hands, like this conversation is draining him, and then reaches across the table to grab my hand. I pull mine back quickly and place it in my lap.

No, no, no! I didn't take a bullet for a cheater.

"My birthday party was a mistake. You and I had not established yet that we were going to be exclusive. Before you, I was never exclusive with anyone—no one ever meant anything to me. At the party, you saw Aurora and I kissing and you stormed off. We had a huge fight and we split up, but I promise you that we talked and worked through all of this. We now have a better understanding of what each other wants and what we can give."

My hands tighten into fists out of frustration. "Please enlighten me, what exactly do we want and what can we give? This doesn't sound like me whatsoever."

"We decided, after you turned down my offer to be lovers, that we would be friends."

So many things are wrong with what he just said. #WTF

"Lovers? Friends? I thought you were my boyfriend?" My head is spinning and I may throw up.

I either have tunnel vision or a bad case of vertigo. I grip the table because my dizziness may cause me to fall out of my seat.

"Elena, this is hard to describe. Our relationship means the entire world to me, but I don't want to lie and tell you that we were something we never officially defined before the shooting. I could lie and say you were my girlfriend. But we never established that." He pauses to look me square in the eyes. "I never did 'friends' with a woman before you. I never did anything official with anyone either. I never did long-term. That was not the man I was or wanted to be. We wrote new rules together for our relationship. But I can tell you this, before the shooting I was ready to make you mine, and then you ran off—"

"I ran off? We fought before the shooting?"

"*Si*. You tried to break up with me out of nowhere and then you ran across the street to flee. The paparazzi noticed me and started taking pictures like crazy, and then the next thing I know you are rushing back across the street screaming at the top of your lungs."

"I wanted to break up with you but I still took a bullet for you? Why?" I didn't mean to say that aloud. *Why can't you just think in your head for once, Elena?*

Even though the question is valid and I do want an answer, I wish I didn't say it to him. Leonardo's face falls, and he looks like I slapped him. I bet he's already been kicking himself thinking the same thing, so why did I have to go ahead and put it in the air between us?

"I'm sorry for being rude. I need to go home now. I'm feeling really dizzy and would like to just lie down and think about all of this. It's a lot to take in. Everything I've been thinking seems to have changed in an instant."

Leonardo doesn't push me to stay longer or to talk anymore. We say *ciao, ciao* to both *Zio* Armando and Abrianna, and then Mateo drops me off at my apartment after a quiet car ride.

6

─────────────

My brain will not shut off. Leonardo dropped me off a few hours ago and I can't sleep. I've tossed and turned in my bed without being able to wrap my head around tonight's dinner conversation.

At 1 a.m. I decide to do what I should have done right away.

"Hello," says a very groggy sounding Sophie over the line.

I didn't take into consideration I'd be calling my best friend at 7 a.m. in Michigan on a Saturday.

"Soph, I need to talk to you."

"Elena, is everything alright?" Her voice becomes clearer, and she's sounding alert. "What's wrong?"

"I had a talk with Leonardo tonight after some woman came into the caffé saying she was my friend. I brought up what she told me to Leonardo at dinner and was pretty surprised what I learned." The words spill out at a rapid speed.

"I'm not sure I understand."

"I confronted Leonardo about an ex-girlfriend named Aurora, who I guess he cheated on me with. Then I found out that we weren't really exclusive, like I assumed we were. Also he says I was breaking up with him before I got shot. And—"

31

"Okay girl, slow your damn roll. Let's start with this so-called friend. Who is she?" Sophie cuts off my endless ranting.

"She said her name was Victoria."

"Victoria! That stupid cunt. I can't believe she's back and messing with you again. You have freakin' amnesia, for crying out loud! I am going to call Delta and get myself a flight out there immediately so I can punch this bitch in her face!"

As Sophie continues to scream vulgarity, I pull the phone away from my face. I've never heard her this fired up before—and I've seen her work some killer deals in a boardroom to land major clients. She kicks ass—but this Victoria person seems to have hit a nerve even with her.

"Soph, I have never heard you call someone the 'c' word before. What has gotten into you? Who is this Victoria chick anyway? I need to understand what's going on. Lucy, you've got some 'splain to do ..."

Sophie pauses before she fills me in on the details. I know this is going to be good; it's rare when she's quiet.

"She's some nasty bitch who was trying to move in on Leo the whole time you were with him. You are definitely *not* friends. She does not like you and you feel the same about her. I've personally never met her but I'd love to. She's a friend of Leo's nasty mom and they weren't nice to you. But I thought you were growing a pair and not caring about what those women have to say about you. And I have no idea about the breakup. You never mentioned that you were thinking about doing that."

"Leonardo's mom doesn't like me?" I whisper. My shoulders slump in defeat.

"Elena, after everything I just said that's what you have a question about? I don't understand why you are still like this."

"Like what?"

"Feeling like you aren't good enough for anyone. You run the world in business, you literally take names and crush competitors, but when it comes to men you never give your heart away because you're always on the defense, acting like you aren't good enough."

"Well when you say it like that I sound like such a catch."

I know she didn't mean to hurt my feelings, but she did. I scan

32

through my past boyfriends and realize, even though I hate to admit it, she's right. I do feel like I don't measure up when it comes to men, even the losers and the cheaters. When I looked at Leonardo in my hospital room, my first thought was how could a guy like him be with a woman like me?

I need therapy, that's for sure.

"Elena, you know I love you! You also know I speak the truth and want the best for you. Listen, I came to Italy after the whole thing went down at the birthday party with Leo and that model whore. You were a mess."

"You did?" I'm shocked to hear this. Sophie came all the way over here just to be with me. #BFF4L

"Hell yes, I did. You didn't think I would let someone upset my best friend without showing up to smack some bitches around?"

I laugh for what feels like the first time today. "So what happened?"

"We went to Milan with Alessandra, you got groped by some creep doctor, we lost you at Juliet's balcony, and we found you helping some lost little boy, and then we went home and you made up with your man."

"Wait—what doctor? What little boy? So much of that sentence makes absolutely no sense."

"Elena, we don't have time to discuss all of that, I have a dentist appointment to get to soon," she says, cutting me off. "But the main thing is Leo must have proved his worth to you in some way. I've never known you to date a guy twice."

She's right there. I do not know how to pick them but I do know not to take them back. But then why did I try to dump him?

It's like she reads my mind when she says, "I know you went to a party with Leo before this apparent break up. You were texting me from the bathroom upset. Victoria and Leo's mom were talking badly about you, but you heard Leo putting them in their place. I'm going to guess you pulled some martyr bullshit and broke up with him because you still didn't think you could be Mrs. Italy, or whatever it would be if you marry Leo."

"Man, this is hard to hear all at once. Thank you for your honesty, Soph. I need to have some time to think all this through."

33

We end our phone call with me promising to call her soon to tell her how I'm feeling. Maybe I should have gone back to Michigan after the hospital? I wouldn't be sitting here so confused if I didn't know any of this happened in the first place.

But that would be quitting, and I am not a quitter.

I don't know why I've never looked at this situation from a business perspective. What would I tell one of my employees if they came into my office bitching about some gossip?

I wouldn't stand for that one bit.

I need to figure this out on my own—no friends, no help from anyone who can only confuse me more. Me, myself, and I.

And if I don't get my memories back, I'll have a set of brand new ones. Also, no more little pity parties. I can't feel bad that this happened to me; I can only look forward.

I'm going to start fresh in Italy, except keep my fun job at Stella's, and see what happens.

A clean slate with everyone—including Leonardo. Or *Leo* as Sophie said.

---

After my little self-help intervention I pulled on myself, I decided to hit the gym Alessandra told me I belong to. If I'm paying for it, I might as well go. Quickly jumping back into my regular treadmill and weight lifting routine gives my life some certainty.

This is something the old Elena knew like the back of her hand. I love working out and it feels good to move my muscles after lying in a hospital bed for days. I'm slower than I'd like but I can't push my body like normal. I know I need to take it easy for awhile, according to Dr. Costa's orders.

When sweat is dripping from every inch of my body, I call it quits and hit the showers. So far, so good. No overwhelming feelings of confusion, regret, or longing—everything I experienced before this morning.

Before there was a looming feeling that something was always missing, and since I have let go of the hope of getting my memories back, I don't have that sense of loss, a loss for the Elena who first came to Italy.

Stepping outside of the gym, I take in my surroundings as if for the first time. Even though it's a large city, it still has a an intimate, romantic vibe. I look next to the gym toward a small square—tables are setup, and at each one I see couples holding hands and looking at each other with adoring eyes.

From the small cars always whipping around in a hurry to the historic ruins—I can't help but to love this place.

I have no plans for the day and I don't have to be at the caffé until the evening shift for our first poetry night—which Marco told me was an idea I was putting together before the shooting.

With time to kill, I explore the streets around me. I avoid the main tourist traps and instead stick to the neighborhoods near the gym. Walking up and down street after street, I take in the sights of the families going about their daily lives, the smells of homemade pasta and bread behind the colorful doors, the wet laundry hanging out the windows to dry, and the rows of houses stacked on top of each other on cobblestone streets.

Somehow, I stumble back upon my own apartment building. I step up the winding stairs to see a ton of brown boxes cluttering the path to my floor. Spotting two guys carrying a large sectional couch up the stairs into the apartment directly across the hall from my own.

The guys have disappeared into the apartment with the couch now, giving me the perfect opportunity to slip into mine without disrupting them. Trying to side step around all the boxes, a man flies out of his apartment and bumps right into me.

Falling off balance, I hit the ground, he grabs me, and I look up into a pair of warm chestnut eyes while I'm in the arms of a stranger.

"I am sorry!" he says in an American accent. His friend, who is standing in the doorway, laughs at the sight of us.

"That's an easy way to meet the neighbors I guess!" his friend says, still laughing and now picking up some of the boxes I tripped over.

I'm still in his arms so I pull back and straighten myself out.

"I'm Brian," the guy who ran into me says as he extends his hand.

"Elena. It's nice meeting you," I say, shaking his hand and Troy's, who I learn is his friend helping him move in.

"Are you American?" I ask, being a little bit nosy.

"Yep, we're from Florida. I was just relocated here for work," Brian says as I study him.

He's very good looking—a few inches taller than me with blond hair and a dazzling white Hollywood smile.

I let them know that I'm from Michigan and working in a local coffee shop not too far from our apartment building. And unlike the former me, who kept my successful company back home a secret, I tell Troy and Brian what I do back home.

Surprisingly, Troy says he's seen me on the cover of *Forbes* in their '30 under 30' issue and has heard of Rock Star Media—he is in marketing too.

Brian lets me know that he's a magazine photographer here on assignment. He's appointed to Rome and many of the surrounding areas in Italy—so he'll be traveling around the country.

I decide to take the lead this time. "I'm not sure if you guys would be into this but there's a poetry night at the coffee shop I work at tonight. If you don't care about poetry I can at least promise you some delicious desserts and coffee!"

They seem like good guys and the idea of making friends with people who know nothing about me before the shooting excites me. It's the fresh start I asked the Universe for.

"We'd love to!" Brian says as Troy eyes him with a smirk.

"We don't know shit about poetry, but we love to eat," Troy adds.

After giving them Stella's address, I excuse myself to get ready for my shift while they clean up the mess they've made in the hallway.

———

Even though I have no memories of organizing poetry night, I'm still on edge hoping everything goes smoothly. It's that obsessive CEO inside of me pushing her way to the surface. I arrive early to the caffé to help Marco setup and take some time to post on the caffé's brand new social media accounts.

I can't believe this little gem tucked away in the heart of Rome doesn't have any way to connect with its loyal customers and to make more.

With or without social media, the place is packed tonight! I'm thankful our loyal customers told all their friends to show up. We've even had to bring out more fold-up chairs from the back, and the espressos and biscotti are flying off the counter.

All of the poets who signed up on our social media pages have shown up and they're ready go. I couldn't be more proud of Stella's.

While I'm behind the counter waiting on customers, Leo walks into the caffè and grabs a spot in line. Even with the place as packed as it is, there's no way to miss his presence. It's been a few days since we last saw each other, after the blow up in *Zio* Armando's restaurant, and I think he's managed to get better looking in our time apart.

He stands taller than everyone else in line. If he wasn't in business, he could surely play professional basketball. I flash him a weak smile, feeling my cheeks heat up, and then quickly turn around to make the drink order I just took.

When Leo strolls to the counter, my heart climbs its way to sit anxiously in my throat. I have to remind myself that I am starting fresh here in Italy and that includes with him. I hope this isn't hard for him to take, but he has to understand the confusion I'm going through.

"*Ciao* Elena, look around," he says, turning his head to take in all the chaos, "this is all because of your hard work. I'm so proud of you!"

His pride for me brings a smile to my face. In a crazy corporate world, it's not often that you are complimented—I'm not used to this.

Leonardo stands to the side, out of the way, to give more seats to the customers, and chats with Marco. When the line shortens, I head to the stage and grab the microphone, tapping it a few times to double check if it's on.

"Test, test," I say, hearing my voice project through the caffè and seeing all eyes turn to me. "I guess this thing really is on! I'd like to welcome you all to Stella's Caffè's first ever poetry night. You're all part of this wonderful caffè's history now. Marco and I are so excited to kick this off, and we hope to make poetry night a regular thing—so plan to come back! Let's welcome to the stage our first poet, Sabrina Carmelo."

The room explodes with applause as I walk back to the counter in case anyone needs a last-minute espresso.

That's when I notice Brian and Troy walk into the caffè. I'm glad to see my new friends decide to show up! I give them a little wave and Troy grabs a table, while Brian heads toward me. I'm sure he's happy to have a new friend in this new country.

"*Ciao*," Brian says in the most American accent you can imagine, making me bust out laughing before I abruptly stop. Sabrina does not need my laughter as a distraction.

"You're definitely going to have to work on that if you want to impress the Italian ladies." I wink.

"Who says I wanted to impress any *Italian* ladies?" he smirks.

Our flirting is light-hearted but I feel a pair of emerald eyes staring intently at me from across the room that I feel like I'm doing something wrong—like I'm cheating on someone whom I have no memories of being with. *But you aren't cheating!* Even with my own pep talk, it doesn't feel right to flirt with Leonardo right here.

"So what can I get you?" I quickly change the subject from women to coffee, hoping that Brian doesn't notice my complete awkwardness.

"I'm not big on coffee, you are going to have to recommend something here."

"Not big on coffee? Are you serious? Next time you better whisper that sentence. In a place like this you could get seriously hurt."

I turn around and whip up two mochas with extra whipped cream on top—hoping to trick these good ol' American boys into loving coffee. Of course, the coffees are on the house.

Brian takes his seat back with Troy and I have a minute to myself to enjoy the poems.

The woman on the stage, Sabrina, pours her heart and soul out, and listening to her makes me teary-eyed. Her poem reflects ending a terrible relationship and how it helped her grow into the woman she is today— strong, confident, and in love with someone else. I'm glad she's found her happily-ever-after despite going through a whole bunch of crap.

I think in the past that would have nauseated me—other people finding love—but I'm surprisingly happy for her.

When Sabrina finishes her poems, she gets a rowdy round of applause and Marco steps up to the microphone to announce the next poet.

There's no one at the register right now, but I remain behind it, wondering if I should go stand by Leo in the back or take a seat at the table with my new neighbor. Why am I worried about this? I'm a grown, single woman—I can sit wherever I damn well please.

But first Leo needs to know that I'm single. I feel like this isn't going to be easy.

I look up from where I was pondering this whole stupid debacle and find Leo standing right in front of the counter.

"Elena, what has you so deep in thought?"

"I think we need to talk, Leo."

"Are you okay?"

"Let's continue this conversation in the back room."

Leo follows me into the back room.

As we stand next to each other near the baking tables, I feel the room suddenly get smaller. I need to pull myself together and just do this. I don't even really know this guy, but I feel like what I'm about to say is heartbreaking.

Leo doesn't say a word; he's just waiting for me to break the silence.

"I'm going to be honest with you, I took it really rough when I heard about the model, the cheating, us not being in a true relationship, and just everything that was dropped on me. I spoke to Sophie and she told me I must have gotten over the whole cheating thing because I was madly in love with you and we were together the last she knew—*after* the scandalous birthday party."

"Elena—" Leo tries to interrupt but I keep my monologue going before I lose my confidence.

"I spent a lot of time thinking about it, and even though she said that I must have forgiven you, I just can't go back to that life. I've been with cheaters before and it's devastating to feel like I'm not good enough. Also, without my memories, I don't want to feel like I'm the one on the outside of some big inside joke. It's causing me anxiety. I have to start fresh here in Italy and I have to be okay with my memories never coming back."

I take a moment to breath, realizing Leo is now pacing back and forth in front of me. His hands shake and he's perspiring. When I'm done speaking, he locks eyes with me and runs his fingers through his thick hair with a look of desperation.

"Elena, where do I fall into this 'starting fresh' plan?"

"I can't be your girlfriend, or whatever it is we were trying to be to get my memories back. I'm not strong enough to do this."

"Please," he paces a few more times, "please don't do this."

"Leo," I try to grab his hands but he's moving around to quick, "I can't change my mind on this. I need to be strong or I'll go crazy. I'm on the verge of having a panic attack every day, just waiting for someone else to drop a bomb on me."

"You ... the old you ... would not want to end this," he pleads.

"I'm not the old me anymore. We can't change that. Let's move past this, please."

Just then Marco rushes into the back room shouting something about biscotti.

"Elena! I've been looking for you for 10 minutes. The poets are taking an intermission and we've got a *grande* line at the counter. I need your help."

I dash out of the back room quicker than Usain Bolt in the Olympics. I need to get away from Leo before I change my mind and run back into his arms—his huge masculine arms.

The rest of the night is luckily chaotic between poets, customers, and Marco that I don't have time to worry about continuing my conversation with Leo or worrying about being rude to Brian and Troy.

Saved by the customers.

# 7

## Leo

Start fresh. What is this bullshit she's talking about? How did I let this happen? I lose my mind waiting for her to gain consciousness in the hospital only for her to wake up and have no memories of me, and now after a stupid fight over old bullshit she wants to be single. Fuck that.

I can't let this happen.

"*Signor Forte,* you have a call on line two, it's your mother."

If this day could get any worse, then it just did.

"*Pronto?*" I greet my mother, who I haven't spoken to since Elena was rushed to the hospital.

She frantically called me when she got wind of the shooting but didn't have the correct information. Mama thought I was the one who was shot. When I told her it was Elena, she didn't seem to care. I basically hung up on her then and we haven't spoke much since.

"I wanted to check on you. How are you doing my boy?"

"Mama, that's not why you called. Can you get to the point? I have a meeting in 15 minutes."

"Leonardo, how can you speak like that to me? This is that American girl's doing. You have never been rude to your mama before."

"Get to the point or I'm hanging up." I push around the files on my desk to find the folders I need for the meeting my mama is surely going to make me show up late to.

"Okay, okay. I'm calling because I need you to come to a foundation meeting tomorrow."

"I don't think I can, this is too short notice."

"I knew you'd say that. I already cleared it with your assistant Natalia last week. You'll be there."

Before I can cut my mom off and give her a piece of my mind for going behind my back, she rushes off the phone claiming she has an incoming call.

Now it's time to let Natalia know she made a grave mistake.

––––––

## Elena

Brian stops by the caffé and sits in one of the cozy chairs near the window, waiting for my shift to end. He said he'd like to check out my gym tonight, and I figure it would be nice to have a buddy. Normally, I like to work out alone, except for when I taught kickboxing classes, then the more the merrier. I hope Alessandra is working tonight; I'd like to introduce her to my new friend.

"Aren't you going to be bored sitting here? I still have about an hour left on the clock," I say, placing a hot chocolate down on his table. He still isn't willing to give espresso a try. I don't blame him; this stuff is strong.

He pulls his laptop out of his black gym bag.

"I'll catch up on some emails and edit photos while I wait. It's no problem. I like it here, it's comfortable, and there's great people watching."

"I agree! Some of these customers are a trip."

I scan the caffè to see if I can point out my fun regulars, but I come up empty.

"And the owner is easy on the eyes too." He smiles back at me.

"I'll let Marco know you think so highly about him." I playfully push on his arm.

Noticing a new customer walk in, I scurry to the counter.

"Elena, how are you? I'm happy you are here!" a tall man with short, dirty blond hair and brown eyes says to me.

He's not one of my regulars and I haven't met him since the shooting.

*Who is this guy?*

Don't tell me this is another one of Leo's exes trying to upset me again.

"I'm great. Thanks for asking. But I'm sorry, do I know you?"

"Ha ha, real funny. I'm sorry for how we ended things. I didn't mean to be rude to you in the Milan nightclub. I was really drunk and let's be honest, you were leading me on."

*Leading him on?*

*Being in a nightclub?*

*Two good-looking men in my life?*

*Me?*

This is another story that sounds nothing like me.

"I'm truly sorry! I don't remember who you are at all." I shrug. I'm getting tired of apologizing for something I have no control over. "I was in a shooting and I have amnesia. I can't remember anything about my time here in Italy. Could I just get you a cup of coffee or something?"

His jaw drops.

Whoever he is, he must not have known about what happened to me. We must not be that close if one of my good friends hasn't told him. Right? Even that crazy woman Victoria knew about my condition.

"Now I feel like a jerk even more than I already did. I had no idea." His entire face changes from a look of anger to compassion.

"My name is Carlo Romano. I'm *Signora Lucca's* doctor. I don't know if you remember her, but I'm going to guess she still comes here daily. She loves you! *Signora* Lucca set us up on a date before—we went out to dinner—and then recently we saw each other again in Milan."

"When I was leading you on and you were rude to me?"

He laughs. "I put my foot in my mouth, as you Americans say, since walking into this caffè. Yes, I was rude to you and I'm sorry. Let's put this behind us."

I pour a regular black coffee into a takeout cup even though he hasn't placed an order. Hopefully he'll take the hint to leave. I don't want to meet any more people from the past I don't remember.

"Well turns out you're in luck. I have to put everything behind me because I can't remember."

I hand him his coffee and realize there's now a line forming behind Carlo—he notices too.

"I'd like to talk to you about what happened to cause your amnesia. I'm concerned for your health." Carlo hands me a business card.

"You can have *Signora* Lucca fill you in—she knows the whole story." I laugh.

He takes my blow off in stride and says *ciao, ciao* so I can take care of my waiting customers.

About 20 minutes later, Marco comes to relieve me from my shift. I toss my green apron into the back room, grab my gym bag, and head over to Brian's table. I know he witnessed the whole ordeal with the doctor, but he doesn't push me for details—which I appreciate.

"Let's blow this popsicle joint," I say, as we leave the caffè for our sweaty destination.

———

My body runs on the treadmill while my mind runs around in circles.

I can't stop thinking about that doctor. Signora Lucca comes in every day, why hasn't she brought him up? Maybe she knows he was disrespectful to me and doesn't want to relive that with me?

I also can't help wondering why I was going on a date with another man since being in Italy. I thought I met Leo right when I got here. Did I have enough time to meet someone else? Did I cheat on him?

Oh my god. If I did then I am the biggest hypocrite. However, that seems completely unlike me.

"Earth to Elena," Brian says, waving his hand in front of my face. "This is Earth paging Elena."

Great, I must have spaced out. I already gave Brian a tour of the gym and now we are on the treadmills working up a sweat.

"I'm so sorry. I'm being a terrible gym buddy," I say, looking over toward my friend.

His face covered in sweat, and he's holding on to the front of his machine for dear life.

"Are you not used to cardio?" I laugh.

"You could say I'm more of a weightlifting type of guy," Brian says between gasps of air.

Before he passes out, I hop off my machine. "Alright big guy, let's go lift weights then!"

"A girl who lifts weights? It's like you've been sent down from heaven," Brian says.

We wipe down our equipment and then he playfully swats my ass with his towel as we head toward the weight room.

Just then I spot Alessandra who gives me a look of utter confusion —she must have witnessed the ass smack with a random guy. She is about to walk into a group exercise class and I tell Brian I'll catch up with him in just a minute.

"Alessandra!" I shout, rushing over to her.

"Elena! Where have you been? Let's go, we are going to be late for class," my beautiful blond friend says as she gets the microphone pack adjusted on her belt.

"I can't take your class today, I'm sorry. I have a friend I'm showing the gym to," I say, nodding in the direction of Brian, "but I did want to ask you a quick question if that's okay?"

"Shoot," she says, still eyeing Brian.

"I know that you, Sophie, and I went to Milan together. Do you remember anything about a doctor being there? Or going to a nightclub?"

"*Sí*, that doctor you went on a date with from your caffé was there for some conference or something. You went off with him in the club

45

that night and came back pissed. Sophie said she saw him trying to get too touchy with you but you fought him off. Good girl."

"I fought off a man in a nightclub? This doesn't sound like me at all." I'm even more confused. "Tell me, when I went on date with him, was I seeing Leo?"

"I don't think so. Leo had just pulled that model bullshit and you blew him off. You went on that date probably to clear your head."

A rush of relief flows through my heart.

I am not a cheater. #ThankGod

"Alright, *bella*, my class is waiting! You better get your booty back in here one day soon." She gives me a double-cheek kiss and heads into the private room.

Brian and I finish our workouts, with me back in the game now that my head isn't in the clouds. I put Brian through a pretty intense weightlifting routine—he had no idea that I used to be a personal trainer. I can't wait to hear him cry about how sore he is tomorrow.

And I'm so glad I don't have to cry from confusion about this doctor any longer.

––––––––

The loudest pounds against my front door wake me from a deep slumber. What time is it? A quick glance at my alarm clock lets me know it's only 7 a.m.!

Who the hell is pounding on my door this early on my day off? This is straight up torture.

The knocking gets louder and louder.

"I'm coming. This better be good!" I swing the door open to end up face-to-face with Brian.

"Well good morning to you too sunshine!" Brian greets me with a smile, holding up a brown bag. "I come bearing gifts. I brought bagels."

"You should have led with the bagels—always lead with the food," I say, letting him into my apartment.

He sits on the stool next to the island in the kitchen while I put on a pot of coffee.

When I turn around, I catch Brian checking me out— staring

intently at my bare legs. I'm wearing the shortest shorts and a sheer tank top, not even a bra. My face must be fifty shades of red right now. I dart to my bedroom before Brian can catch a glimpse of anything else, and I throw on a bra and a hoodie for good measure.

"I promise I don't welcome all my neighbors to the building with a peep show like that!" I try to break the ice when I walk back into the kitchen.

Brian is now eating an everything bagel, and I notice a plain one on a plate waiting for me.

"I think most of our neighbors are senior citizens. You'd definitely give *Signor* Moretti down the hall a heart attack if he saw those gorgeous legs! But I can't say that I mind the peep show welcome one bit," Brian laughs as he takes the coffee I'm handing him. "I was wondering if you wanted to explore Rome with me today?" He says the words quickly, looking down at his bagel the entire time.

Is he nervous? We just hung out yesterday. Is this different? *Maybe it's a date?*

I know I should be excited to spend time with people who didn't know me before the shooting, so I accept his offer. However, I find myself fighting a nagging voice in the back of my head reminding me of a handsome Italian man who was pleading for my attention at poetry night.

But that doesn't mean I should ignore my perfectly nice handsome neighbor.

"*Perfecto*! Wait ... is that Spanish?" Brian jokes getting up from the bar stool and tossing out the rest of his bagel.

"*Si,* that was *espanol mi amigo.* In Italian, it's *perfetto.* We'll work on your Italian so you don't want to stick out like a sore thumb. These Italians will eat you alive!"

Brian and I agree that we'll meet in the hallway between our apartments in an hour. I rush to pull together a cute outfit to wear for my sightseeing date. Is this a date? I don't even know.

Screw it; let's just get ready.

## 8

---

Jumping on a crammed bus with a bunch of fellow tourists, we head straight to the Vatican City. The warm summer weather brings people from all over the world to the Eternal City. iPhones and selfie sticks (yes, those are real things) are out, ready to capture the historical country.

Yes, the Vatican is its own country. #Fact

When the bus stops, we file out into a packed crowd waiting in St. Peter's Square. I notice a young blond woman gathering a group together outside the *Musei Vaticani*—or Vatican Museums—and ask her if we still have time to join her tour.

She welcomes us and says her name is Melanie, and she's from South Carolina. Turns out she has her master's degree in art and found herself here in Italy after graduating, never looking back. Now that sounds like fun and much more responsible than leaving behind your million-dollar company.

This reminds me to send Sophie a 'thank you' gift for keeping things afloat back in Detroit. I don't know what I'd do without my best friend.

Brian and I stick together during Melanie's tour, listening to all the facts about Renaissance art. Miles of art, sculptures, and tapestry sit inside the Vatican Museums.

However, I can't help but notice something in the rooms featuring Greek and Roman statutes: the male penises. Fig leaves cover them and some are just broken off. Melanie says that during a certain time period hundreds of years ago the naked body was looked at as "dirty" or "damaged" and the statutes were covered up. Poor dudes.

The thought of seeing a certain Italian man's cock comes to mind. I instantly blush and feel like everyone in this room must know my dirty thought about Leo.

*Why are you thinking of him right now?*

I look over at Brian who is standing awfully close to me. I'm not sure if it's because we are packed in here like sardines or he just wants to be near me. I get my answer though, when he holds my hand. I don't want to make the rest of the day awkward so I leave my hand in his.

It doesn't feel too bad placed in mine.

After a few more rooms, we are all shuffled into the Sistine Chapel. My eyes instantly dart to the infamous ceiling; I let out a small gasp in disbelief as I walk into the room backwards with my head toward the sky. My eyes can't take in the whole sight at once, but I don't want to miss anything. Michelangelo's *The Last Judgment* and Creation of Adam are breath taking. I crane my neck to see it all.

When we walk out of the chapel our tour ends. We tip Melanie because she was absolutely fabulous! And I let her know about Stella's Caffé—telling her if she ever stops in, she's got an espresso on the house waiting for her.

Now that our big group splits up, I notice the silence between Brian and me and that my hand is still warmly placed in his.

I self-consciously look at my travel companion and say, "Where to next?

"I'm thinking ... *gelato.*"

"I'm thinking you just said my favorite Italian word. *Andiamo.*"

On our way out of the hectic Vatican City we head toward the Spanish Steps to make a quick pit stop before our gelato, jumping into the ship-like Barcaccia Fountain.

Climbing inside, I stand on the step designed for cupping your hands under the stream, and take a big sip of water.

Now finally, *gelato*. A few side streets over we find a *gelato* bar. Placing our orders at the counter inside, we then bring our desserts outside to sit on the Spanish Steps.

As the day warms up, I'm thankful that I put sunscreen on this morning! I would be burned to a crisp by now.

"I think I've died and gone to heaven," I say as I lick my mouthwatering hazelnut gelato.

"This is the best ice cream I've ever had!" Brian agrees. We sit together finishing our gelato and chat about what life is like living in Rome. He tells me a little more about his photography work and what he's looking forward to seeing in the country.

"And what about guys? Have you seen anyone since coming to Italy?" Brian takes the conversation into a zone I'm not too comfortable talking about just yet.

"Nothing serious." I try to blow off the question. I know it's technically a lie but what I don't remember shouldn't be held against me.

"Well that makes me feel better. Now I know I can safely do this." Brian leans in and gently kisses me. His lips feel soft and nice across my own. It's nothing like Zack's kisses, the only kisses I can remember, as he was super sloppy. Too much tongue.

We pull apart, and to avoid any further questions about my romantic life, I get up to throw our napkins in the nearby trashcan when I feel the hairs on the back of my neck stand up.

A chill runs down my body, even though it's a blistering hot day. I'm suddenly very aware of my emotions, feeling like something is wrong. Scanning the area, I don't see anything or anyone that looks out of place—just tourists going about their day, taking pictures, and talking quickly in a million different languages.

But I swear I'm being watched. I just know it.

Could this be what the doctor described as a Post Traumatic Stress Disorder moment? I know the doctor told me that I could experience PTSD with what happened to me, but I clearly ignored his warnings.

"Hey! Are you okay, Elena? You look like you've seen a ghost." Brian comes up behind me and placing his hand on my shoulder.

"Yes, I'm so sorry," I say. "I felt like I was being watched."

I've been able to avoid telling him about the shooting, but now that it's made me look crazy, I have to explain. So I give him a quick recap, and he looks at me in utter shock.

"I can't believe you went through all that and you're going out-and-about right now in giant crowds. I give you credit for being this brave."

"Brave?" I shake my head. "I don't feel brave. Actually, I feel very dumb because I didn't even think about my safety in crowds until right now."

Wow, how could I be so careless? This isn't like me.

"If you want to head back home, I completely understand. I don't want you to feel unsafe," Brian says. I see him take a look as his grip on my shoulder gets a little tighter.

On the walk back to our apartment building, I remain pretty silent. A few words escape my lips. I have to be honest, my thoughts keep replaying the scared feeling from the Spanish Steps.

Brian walks with his arm draped around my shoulder the whole way. I'm thankful he's here right now—I desperately need a friend.

As we walk into our building, a black town car pulls up in front of the door.

"Elena." I squint to see Leo's driver, Mateo, get out of the car.

I haven't heard from Leo since the poetry night, when I told him we couldn't be together anymore and then blew him off hiding behind my work.

"Do you know that man?" Brian asks.

"Yes, it's okay, Brian. I'll just run over to chat with him real quick. Thank you so much for such a fun day—from the bagel to the gelato!"

He leans in and plants a quick kiss on my cheek.

"I had fun too!" he says before leaving me standing on the steps outside the building.

I walk over to Mateo, who saw the cheek kiss. I feel guilty, as he has no idea about the earlier lip lock. Why do I feel guilty? I'm a single girl.

"*Ciao Mateo, come esta?*"

"Elena, are you okay?" His words always come out so powerful, but his voice is quiet I need to stand close to hear him.

"Yes, I'm fine." I do not make eye contact.

I'm not okay; I just freaked out in a public place in front of my new friend. I may not remember anything about Italy, but I do remember what fear feels like.

"Elena, I don't want to alarm you, but Leo got a threatening note in the mail to his personal house. The letter did mention you as well. Leo wants me to be your personal bodyguard until this crazy person is caught and behind bars. I saw you at the piazza today. What happened?"

I feel like I'm hit by a brick. A threatening letter that includes my name ... to Leo's house ... a personal bodyguard ... seeing my freak out.

Wait a second.

"Have you been following me Mateo?" This time I lock eyes with the salt-and-pepper-haired man. I can tell I just caught him in what could have been a lie, but he's lucky his sunglasses hide his full expression.

"I may have been."

"For how long? Be honest."

"Since you left the hospital."

"What?"

"And did you know I was there?"

Oh my god. No, I didn't know he was there. Today isn't the first time I've been followed. My *gelato* inches up my throat. I lean out a trashcan on the street and throw up.

I am not safe here. Should I go home? No, danger lurks everywhere. *And Leo is not back home.* Whoa, whoa, calm down crazy inner voice, where did that come from?

"Mateo, I see your point. As much as it makes me feel uncomfortable to have a personal bodyguard, I'll accept your help."

"*Grazie, Signor Forte* wouldn't have it any other way."

Still standing on the sidewalk, I launch into the explanation of what happened at the Spanish Steps. I have no concrete details, just a feeling. I probably sound insane, but Mateo reassures me that I'm not. He says I should trust my intuition, making me feel a little better.

He explains to me what he's been doing in his routine to 'watch over' me (as he called it) and we set up something more official. He also gives me his phone number so I can contact him if I feel scared or unsafe.

I don't normally accept help, especially from bossy men like Leo, but it touches my heart that he cares about my safety. Even after I said all that stuff in the coffee shop to push him away, he still cares, and I care that he cares

Okay, maybe I am insane.

## 9

**Leo**

Incoming email: mateo@forteenterprises.com
Here are the photos you asked for from my surveillance on Elena.

Attached I find a ton of photos showing Elena with that man from poetry night. I quickly flip past the photos of them at the museum and Sistine Chapel, looking too cozy for my liking.

How can she be with this chump? What does he have to offer her? She's worth much more than this guy.

*Has she kissed him yet? Fucked him? I'll kill him if he's touched my woman in that way.*

I didn't ask Mateo for these pictures to spy on her date—I'd rather not even see. My blood boils at the sight of her smiling with another man.

What I really want to find are the photos from the Spanish Steps. Flipping through a few more pictures, the ones I want immediately jump out. Elena looks terrified, her face drained of those usually rosy cheeks. That girl is always blushing. It pains me to see her like this.

Scanning through each and every picture, I find nothing. I look for any familiar faces or anything out of place. Nothing. I know Mateo did the same thing. He's been watching her since she left the hospital and has had nothing to report.

I flip to a photo that makes me feel full of rage, like I could flip my fucking desk right now. He's kissing her. And she's letting him. *Stronzo.* I need to get her back so she can stop wasting her time and kisses with this asshole.

Jealousy is not an emotion I'm familiar with.

Spying on her should make me feel bad, but I desperately want to keep her safe. Assigning her a bodyguard was my way of allowing another person, who I trust with my life, to know her whereabouts and not me. I felt like she'd agree with me on this.

Whoever shot my girl and took her memories away is going to pay.

I will find them and I will kill them.

No one hurts what's mine.


**Elena**


Later that night I'm in the kitchen making a quick marinated chicken breast and vegetable salad when my phone beeps, indicating a text message.


*"Mateo told me about the Spanish Steps. Are you okay, cara?"*


My heart skips a beat to see Leo's term of endearment in the text message. I send off a quick reply.

.   .   .

55

*"You mean the 24/7 stalker you set up without letting me know? lol Thank you for that. I am okay now, just got scared."*

*"I don't want you to ever feel scared. Call me next time something like this happens, please."*

*"You don't have to worry about me."*

*"Are you kidding me? You saved my life. I will do anything to protect yours. I owe you the world."*

Staring down at my phone, I don't know what to say next. I don't think I've ever been at a loss for words, ever.

I wish I could remember what it was like being that woman who jumped in front of that bullet. And, even more, I wish I could remember the love that woman felt for the man she took the bullet for.

Before I have a chance to collect my thoughts, he sends another text message.

*"Can I see you?"*

*"I have an early morning at the caffé & it's getting late. I don't think that would be a good idea."*

*"Tomorrow then?"*

Do I want to see him? I tried to push him out. Is there a way to collect new memories *with* him without worrying about the past ones I'm forgetting—good and bad?

I guess I won't know if I don't try.

*"Ok, tomorrow."*

*"Grazie bella. I'll pick you up for dinner at your apartment around 8pm."*

I finish my salad, plop down on the couch, and throw on some mindless reality show on Netflix. Now this I remember. And this is boring. No wonder I escaped.

———

"Oh my God, Marco. This Italian rum cake is absolutely amazing!"

"You actually came up with that recipe."

"Say what?" I nearly break my neck whipping it around quickly to stare at him in complete astonishment. "I did?"

We're catching up on each other's lives while drinking espressos and eating an early lunch before our busy rush starts.

*"Si,* we were experimenting one day and you came up with it. You started off a mess when it came to baking, but you got brave in the kitchen after a while."

There's that word again—brave. I've never been brave, unless it's in a boardroom and I'm fighting for my company or clients. When I walk out those doors, that mask comes down.

"So tell me, who were those two American guys you were talking to at poetry night?" my nosy friend asks before taking a bite of his sandwich.

"The one is my new neighbor, Brian, and the other is his friend who was helping him to move in, Troy. They're from Florida."

"And ...?"

"And what?"

"And you seemed very friendly with them."

"Is this an interrogation? You would have made a great cop Marco." I laugh. "You sure you don't want to make a career change?"

He frowns and puts down his sandwich. "If you're going to change the subject, we are going to at least talk about that heated conversation between you and Leo I accidentally walked into. I'm sorry about that the other night, but I needed your help."

This guy knows how to drill questions. Damn, he doesn't miss a beat. I look away and then look back at Marco.

"Fine. Brian and I seemed very friendly because we are *friends*. And I was telling Leo that I couldn't be with him anymore. I can't take the stress of not having my memories and the only way I'm going to survive here in Italy is if I start fresh—from everything."

"Oh Elena, I'm sorry that this whole crazy experience had to happen to you. You fought so hard for your relationship with Leo and for it to be taken away from you makes me sad."

This sounds very similar to what Sophie has been saying to me about my relationship as well. Everyone seems to be pulling for us as a couple— is there something there I can't see?

"But Marco, just from the way other people have been describing our relationship, it sounds like I was the only one fighting?"

He waits a minute before saying, "I can't speak for Leo because I didn't know him well before the shooting, but when he was out of your life you were very gloomy. We talked a lot about your relationship. When he was in it, you were ecstatic."

Our conversation is cut short when the lunch hour strikes and customers start lining up out the door on their breaks from work.

The rest of my shift is full of Americanos with extra shots of espresso, macchiatos with whipped cream, iced lattes, and cappuccinos with milk.

I appreciate when there's no time to talk about hunky Italian men begging to be in my life.

———

The doorbell rings as I'm curling my last piece of hair. I know I have naturally curly hair, but I decided to change it up tonight with long, loose curls.

I even bought a new dress from a local boutique I pass on my way home every day. The girl at the counter seemed to recognize me. Maybe I've been there before? I didn't ask because I don't care to know what else I'm missing.

The dress is cute—black and white that stops mid-thigh, it's fitted on top but flowing out toward the bottom. Paired with gorgeous purple open-toed pumps, I feel confident in my appearance, but nervous for everything else.

Butterflies, definite butterflies.

*You don't feel butterflies when you're with Brian.*

Inner thoughts—why do you sneak up on me when I don't want you there?

Even though Leo didn't call it a date, I decided to treat it like one.

A *first* date, to be exact.

I want to go into tonight as if I were on a blind date where the two people know absolutely nothing about each other.

This man hasn't cheated on me, I haven't lost my mind over him because I'm confused or angry, and no one saved the other person's life —no expectations whatsoever.

I hope that's okay with Leo. He has a private bodyguard following me around without my initial permission, the least he can do is pretend to go on a blind date with me.

A knock on the front door pulls me out of the clouds.

Opening it, I nearly drop my jaw upon seeing how dashing Leo looks standing in the small hallway. The way his black and grey suit hugs his firm frame is definitely eye candy.

"Elena, you look mesmerizing." Leo hands me a bouquet of long-stemmed red roses—my favorite!

Did he know that?

*Forget about that Elena, no questions about what he already knows.*

I step inside to put them in a vase, and Leo doesn't take his eyes off me the entire time. Grabbing my purple Louis Vuitton clutch, we head out the door together.

And that's when we bump, yes physically bump, right into Brian.

Embarrassment shines on my red face as Brian stares between Leo and me.

Leo must recognize Brian from the caffé, and sensing a threat, he puts his hand on my lower back.

*A display of his property?*

Kind of arrogant and kind of hot at the same time.

"Elena, it's nice to see you again. I tried to check on you this morning but you must have been at the caffé. Is everything okay? I didn't feel comfortable leaving you with that older man the other day after our date. I should have stayed with you," Brian says, standing taller and locking eyes with Leo. #Showdown

If one of them lifts his leg to pee on me, I will kill him.

"Yes, thank you, Brian. Mateo is my bodyguard— you'll probably see him around. Or maybe not? He's like a ninja." I laugh, trying quickly to end this conversation.

I move closer to the stairs, hoping Leo will follow, but just then Brian sticks out his hand and introduces himself to Leo.

The two men make brief introductions and then stare back at me. I must look like a deer in headlights just staring back. A lot of staring going on in this small hallway.

*Is it getting hot in here?*

"We have reservations at 8:30—we really need to go." Leo finally breaks the awkward silence.

"It was nice to see you again, Brian," I say before sprinting down the stairs with Leo close behind.

That's a coward move to leave Brian in the hallway; I need to clear the air between us when I get back by letting him know that I'm not interested in that way. It would be nice to be romantic with someone new, but I can't force feelings that don't exist.

As soon as I get inside the backseat of the town car next to Leo, he says, "He likes you."

"He's just my friend," I quickly reply, looking out the window as Mateo drives us away.

"Does he know that? And what were you two doing the other day?"

"Listen, I don't need to defend myself to you. Remember the whole 'starting fresh' thing I'm trying to do," I say, clearly realizing that being in this car right now makes me look like a liar on that front, but I still hold my ground.

"I'm sorry, *bella*. It's very hard for me to see you with another man. What's mine is mine."

"And you don't think it was easy for me to see you with another woman?"

"But you don't even remember that!" Leo slams his fist into the car door.

If steam could come out of someone's ears, then Leo would be fuming right now. I feel bad for saying what I did. I don't remember and it's not fair to keep bringing up the past, over and over again.

"Now I'm the one that's sorry." I put my hand on his thigh to comfort him. "No, of course, I don't remember. But me wanting to start fresh means I'm giving us a clean slate. It's only fair. Can we pretend like this a blind date?" I chuckle, hoping to break up some of the anger in the air between us.

"A blind date? I've never been on a blind date before."

"I'd love to be your first," I wink at him, a little more daring in my flirtations now.

"I'd love for you to be my first too. So how do we do this?" He puts his large warm hand on top of mine, which is still resting on his muscular thigh.

"Let's pretend we haven't met before and take it from there. What would you say to me if you just met me?"

"I told you I wanted to fuck you and find out if your cherry red lips taste as good as they look," he says with a growl.

I squeeze my thighs together, feeling a pull between my legs.

"You said that to me?"

"*Si, cara* I told you exactly what I wanted from the start and you shot your sassy comments back at everything I said. You were a tough challenge, but well worth it."

Damn it memories, come back from outer space, will you.

"Did we ... *fuck?*" I boldly ask. I don't think I've ever said the word fuck in this context in front of anyone before.

"Oh yes, we fucked."

Okay now my panties are officially soaked and my breasts may even be a little tender. My nipples are definitely hard beneath this dress just thinking about him fucking me. Good thing I've got a padded push-up bra on—he can't see the reactions he's getting out of me.

I lean back in the seat, turning openly to Leonardo. "You know what, talking about past fucking with a stranger is not appropriate," I say, getting back into the blind date role. "So Mr. Forte, tell me what a day in your life is like?"

"Is this a date or an interview?" he asks, throwing a shit-eating grin back.

"How do you know I'm not a journalist? We've just met and you haven't asked me what I do for a living yet."

"Okay, *cara*, I'll play along with your game if it makes you smile like that." Leo takes his hands off me. "A day in the life is different each and every day. But typically I wake up, drink an espresso like every other Italian man, eat the breakfast my chef Gemma made, I'll hit the gym— I own two by the way— and then I'll go into the office to break some balls."

"Then what?"

"I like to stop in this little caffé that has a beautiful owner, it's called Stella's. I don't know if you've heard of it? I used to date this woman, she is my everything, but she's sitting in this car right now pretending we don't know each other."

Before I can reply about how sweet that sounds, he continues.

"I'm okay with playing her games if it means I'm one step closer to getting between those silky thighs again, making her scream my name in pleasure while I'm eating her tight pussy. That's where I, and only I, belong."

"Leo," I say, breathlessly.

"I don't think I told you my name, *miss?*"

Okay, well two can play at this game.

"Don't you want to know about my day?" I don't even wait for him to reply before I launch into my answer. "A typical day in America for me would have been ... starting my mornings with a protein shake and catching up on endless emails. Before I pull my hair out over something crazy happening in the office, I take out some frustration in the gym—I don't own any if you were wondering."

Leo chuckles.

"Then I'll head into my office where my assistant will give me a rundown of the day. Like yours, it's always different. Interviewing new clients, meetings with current clients, and constantly on the lookout for new opportunities. I eat lunch at my desk, never stopping to look up from the computer or smartphone. Then I head home for dinner—which is by myself or the last I can remember was with my boyfriend, Zack. I guess *ex-boyfriend* Zack is more like it."

"You didn't mention anything about ending your night fucking this Zack?"

The way his Italian accent says the name Zack makes it sound even more douche-like.

Take that, Zack.

"I, uh," I mutter, not entirely sure how to answer him.

"You're stalling." Leo cocks his head to the side.

I'm surprised by his question and the honesty behind it. But I guess Leo has been very straightforward with me—except for the whole pretending he didn't kiss someone else thing—it shouldn't catch me off guard.

"To be honest, I don't think I've ever *fucked* someone. Definitely not Zack," I say with a laugh. "Zack was the worst in bed! All my ex-boyfriends were terrible, or at least they never made me feel sexy enough to let go and truly enjoy myself. I highly doubt any of them ever noticed I never had an orgasm." #Faker

"You've had many orgasms with me, *bella.*"

"If I don't remember them, then they don't count," I say, with my own smirk this time, trying to keep my cool after I just made myself look like an idiot.

"Give me another chance to prove it to you and your body."

Before I can take him up on his offer, Mateo rolls down the divider and lets us know we are at our destination.

Mateo steps out of the car and walks around to open the door for me, gently taking my hand and leading me to the sidewalk.

Leo stands at my side in an instant. The two men exchange words about when to pick us up, and I'm led inside a spectacular underground restaurant that looks like an old wine cellar. Candles and twinkle lights illuminate the room, delicate beige cloths cover wooden tables, and a live band plays classic Italian love songs near the back.

We are escorted by a cute young brunette hostess to our table and given iPads as menus. Our waiter quickly strolls to our table and Leo orders two glasses of red wine and an appetizer of oysters for us to share.

"Oysters, huh? Isn't that supposed to be some kind of kinky aphrodisiac?"

"You have a dirty mind, but if you want them to lead to something kinky, I can make that happen," he says.

"Not in a public restaurant. You're supposed to be a gentleman." Leo laughs so hard that people at other tables look over at us. I don't think I've ever seen him laugh this deeply.

"Did I say something funny?"

"*Cara,* you have no idea all the public places we've fooled around. I am no gentleman," he says, calming down and regaining his stoic composure.

*We've had sex in public?*

*Am I insane?*

We are both public figures who can easily be watched—why would we risk something like that? *Because it sounds sexy as sin!*

"Tell me, where?" I lean into the table.

"Are you sure you want to know? You said we weren't going to talk about the past."

"Tell me."

I'm too intrigued by this wild woman I have become, and forgotten, since getting to Italy and meeting this charming man. I can't picture myself doing anything like what he's describing.

"In two night clubs, a swimming pool, and boutique dressing room." He stops to think if there's more and my face heats up. Despite embarrassment, my body tingles at the thought of sex with him.

"Okay that's enough, you don't have to tell me if there's any more. I find this hard to believe. I am not this girl. I feel like you knew someone else." I meet his eyes semi-embarrassed of this confession.

"She's in there, deep inside you, waiting to come out and play with me again," he says, slightly licking his lips.

"Here's your wine," our waiter says, showing up to bring a relief of much needed alcohol and oysters. He takes our dinner orders and then quickly escapes back to the kitchen.

Needing a distraction, I take a large gulp of my wine. It's dry, which I normally dislike, but at this point I don't give a crap—I want to drown in this glass. I'm angry that I don't remember all this hot sex, and now I'm horny in hopes of having more.

*Having more? I want to have sex with him again? Fuck yes, I do! But it's your first date!*

While I've been having an inner battle, Leo has an oyster ready to eat. Watching him tip his head back and slip the oyster from the shell into his mouth, it does something to me. He licks his lips and places the shell on his plate. Damn ... those lips are so sexy. I want them all over my body, right now, at this table.

*I thought you didn't do it in public places?*

Shut up inner voice—you let me be a slut in the past.

My turn! I pick up an oyster shell, tip my head back, and slowly pour it into my mouth. It's slightly salty but I swallow it and then suck my bottom lip into my mouth. Biting down on it, I sure hope this is sexy to him. I've never tried to seduce a man before, that I can remember anyway.

Leo adjusts himself into a new position in his seat. *It's working!*

"*Signor* Forte, you look uncomfortable. Are you okay?" I coo at him in a whisper across the table.

"I'm hard for you and I want to take you across this table."

There's that honesty again and he's definitely not a gentleman like I thought. I put my elbows on the table and lean in toward him, putting my breasts on display.

"Do you like what you see?"

He eyes grow dark and I swear I hear him growl under his breath. Actually growl, like a beast.

"I see you know what you're doing to me and if you don't stop we are going to fuck in the bathroom or we will be leaving right now."

*Stop? This is way too much fun!*

Just then I get an idea.

"Excuse me, I need to use the bathroom real quick."

I stride toward the ladies room with my newfound confidence. I walk into a stall and slip my black thong panties down my legs and ball them up in my hand. I leave the stall and take a quick look at myself in the mirror. I don't even recognize this woman but she looks happy ... and sexy. Glowing actually.

Walking back toward our table with my little gift hidden in my hand gets me excited. I head toward Leo's side of the table, realizing he's changed his seat. He's now sitting directly next to me. I stick the panties into his jacket pocket and whisper in his ear, "These are for you."

I fight the urge to bite down on his earlobe.

Leo takes the panties out of his pocket, keeping them under the table only for his eyes to see, and then he looks back up at me.

"Finish your wine, *cara*."

Just when I think I've won this little game, a strong hand grasps my thigh under the table. He keeps it there, not moving it an inch while I pick up my wine glass, and just as I'm about to take a sip he slowly drags his hand up my thigh toward my sex, my hungry sex ready to skip this dinner and eat him alive.

Squeezing my thighs together, I trap his hand and chug the rest of my wine.

He pushes my thighs apart and continues his crawl up my inner thigh. Slow and tortuous. The combination of the wine, his hand, and working myself up over this moment has my skin flushed. I'm on fire.

Leo's hand reaches my pussy and he drags a finger through my folds.

I'm wet for him and he knows it.

"Leo, we are in public," I say, breathlessly in a whisper, trying not to draw attention to our table. We are sitting in the middle of the room, surrounded by other couples.

"You started this, Elena. And now I am going to finish it."

Before I can argue, he pinches my clit and I knock my thankfully empty wine glass over. The couple at the table next to ours stares at me and I just laugh it off; hopefully they'll chalk it up to me looking like I'm trashed.

Relentless in his pursuit, Leo circles my clit with my juices and my legs shake. I grab on to the tablecloth with my fist, trying not to display the absolute pleasure I'm feeling across my telling face.

"Elena, you look a little flushed?" Leo teases me.

But before I can retort back a smart ass comment, he sticks a finger inside my pussy. I'm hypersensitive right now, feeling every single emotion on overdrive.

Leo slowly works his finger in and out of my entrance, pushing me toward my limit. I'm about to explode and black out.

Letting out a quiet moan, I shut my eyes. Just then Leo pulls his fingers out of my core and flicks his finger over my sweet spot.

Unable to control myself, I orgasm all over his hand.

Keeping my eyes closed for a minute longer, I barely open them in time to spot our waiter heading toward our table.

If he had shown up a minute sooner, then he would have seen me in the height of my ecstasy.

"I can't believe we just did that." I make eye contact with the beautiful Italian man at my side.

He takes his hand out from under the table, and slowly brings a finger to his mouth and sucks on it.

*Fuck that was hot.*

"Spinach risotto."

"That's me," Leo says.

We have the rest of our meals, dessert, and after dinner espresso in comfortable conversation.

We drop the game of 'pretend it's our first date' and I notice how much I enjoy his company. He makes me feel confident about myself— except when it comes to the sex talk, of course. We chat about our latest projects at work, he asks about Marco and Alessandra, and I tell him more about my last memories before coming to Italy.

I can easily see how my pre-amnesia self fell smitten for this man.

―――――

As we step out of the restaurant, a cameraman spots us heading to the car and rushes over to us. It's dark out and the bright camera flashes causes me to stumble. Gripping onto Leo, he wraps his arm around me and pulls me into his chest.

Flash after flash after flash goes the paparazzi camera.

"Leo! Elena! Any word about your shooter?" The pap shouts.

He's standing entirely too close, I can smell the garlic on his breath.

We don't answer him but that doesn't stop him from asking more questions.

"Are you nervous to be on the streets of Rome alone now? Will you pose for a photo?"

More flashes.

Mateo pulls the car up to the curb, and we dash inside the back-seat. I'm grateful that the car windows are tinted.

"I apologize. I didn't know you had finished eating." Mateo looks at us through the rearview mirror.

"It's not your fault, Mateo. I should have texted you to let you know. I figured Elena and I could take a walk down the street, it's my fault," Leo says back to his faithful friend in a surprisingly calm voice.

Leo pulls me closer to him. I'm practically in his lap now, but this feels perfect. Like it's my spot. I feel safe in this strong man's arms.

"Elena, you're shaking. Are you okay *la mia amore?*"

My love. My heart melts a little in hearing him say that.

"Yes, just got a little startled, I guess." I nuzzle my head into his neck. "The other day I completely forgot I should be on alert for my safety and now maybe I'm too aware of my surroundings."

"I will never let anyone hurt you again," he says, pulling me even tighter against him, "I give you my word."

I cuddle into his warm chest and we drive back to my apartment in silence, remaining in each other's arms.

————

We pull up outside my apartment, and Leo walks with me until we reach my door. I smile up at him—my protector—and thank him for a lovely dinner. I want to thank him for a lovely orgasm as well, but I decide right now is not the time for my "smart mouth"—as he likes say.

Leo leans in and plants a soft kiss on my cheek.

"My pleasure. When can I see you again?" Tomorrow?

I want to ask him to come in but I think that's a little forward, even though he fingered me at the dinner table.

"Tomorrow can't come soon enough." Leo plants a kiss on the other cheek. "Goodnight, *bella*."

## 1 0

---

*Again with this early morning shit?*

Glancing over at my alarm clock, I see it's 6 a.m. and the loud banging at the front door is back. Why me! I drag myself from my warm bed and this time take a look at my sleepwear— you never know who's at the door.

With black yoga pants and a T-shirt on, I head toward whoever is pounding on the front door.

The knocking does not let up.

Peaking through the peephole, I spot two police officers. Maybe they caught the shooter!

I swing open the door, a little too excited.

"Good morning *Signora* Scott, I'm officer Barsotti and this is officer Adessi."

"Come in officers. Would you like some coffee?"

They take me up on the offer for coffee—like any good Italian should—and I invite them into the kitchen area of my open floor plan apartment.

"We came because we wanted to give you an update on our investigation into the shooting," officer Adessi says while taking a sip of his black coffee. "We are currently having the note that was delivered to *Signor* Forte analyzed for fingerprints."

"I realize now I've never asked what that note said." Again with my carelessness.

"It said—'I've been watching you and your little girlfriend too'—and it was on a white card in a white envelope written in black ink. No return address, of course. *Signor* Forte said he didn't recognize the handwriting. We should have brought it for you. If you want to come to the police station, then we could show you."

*I've been watching you.*

Chills run down my body and I have goose bumps, I knew I was being watched. I sit down on one of the bar stools, realizing I may pass out.

"I can't go to the police station today, I have a shift at the caffé in about an hour. Can I come after?"

"*Si,* you can come anytime you'd like," officer Barsotti says.

"Are there any leads?"

I know from Mateo and Leo that they don't have any—I think the guys are in contact with the police every day—but I have to ask out of my own curiosity.

"We have a few leads that have come through our tip line but they need to be checked out because most have turned up empty. We won't know until we do a little more police work though," officer Barsotti says.

"*Grazie* for coming to give me an update. I truly appreciate that."

They hand me their cards and let me know that I can call them if I think of anything or need any help. I escort them out of my apartment, wash their coffee cups, and stroll to the shower to get ready for work. Even though I got a full night's sleep, I'm dragging ass now. Exhausted and scared.

*Snap out of it! You've never acted like you're a victim when life throws you a curveball.*

Curveball? No, life shot a bullet at me. *At Leo.*

I need to ask him tonight who is bodyguarding him since he's given me his main man, Mateo.

My shift goes by peacefully and I'm starting to recognize regular customers again. *Signora Lucca* comes in every day to check on how I'm doing and to ask if I've gotten my memories back yet.

I sadly have to tell her 'no' each and every day, but I find her comforting in her pursuit. I'm glad to have people in my life who care about me.

When my shift is nearing its end a teenage boy dressed in a messenger's outfit comes into the caffé asking for me. With a smile, he hands me a red envelope.

*Could this be from the shooter?*

*Could this be the shooter?*

I drop the envelope as all the color drains from my face.

"Elena, Elena. Are you okay?" Marco asks, picking the envelope up off the floor.

"Open it please, Marco," I whisper with my eyes locked on the door of the caffé.

*Why did I let the messenger leave?*

"Are you sure you want me to open it?"

"Yes! Just do it, please!"

Marco does what I ask and opens the envelope and then his frown turns into a grin. "I think you're going to want to read this yourself," he says, handing me it back.

*Bella*

*Mateo is waiting outside to start tonight's adventure! I will meet you at the end of your scavenger hunt—if you can find me. Can't wait to see you!*

*Your amore,*

*Leo*

*PS—Ditch the panties*

My face heats up with the line about the panties. I look up to meet

Marco's eyes and we both start laughing. Of course, he read that part too.

"He's smooth! I think if I told a lady to 'ditch her panties' she'd slap me," Marco says in between catching his breath from laughing.

"You just haven't found the right lady to say it to yet!"

Marco is a great guy. I need to find him a lady friend, and he deserves it for sure.

"What are you standing around here for? Go out and start your adventure!" Marco practically shoves me out of the caffè and into Mateo's waiting arms.

Mateo turns around from the driver's seat smiling. I don't think I've ever seen Mateo smile like this before.

"Are you ready, Elena?"

"*Sì!* Let's get this party started, Mateo!" I giggle.

I don't think I've been this excited over something in a long time. My stomach flutters with excited nerves.

Mateo drives for 10 minutes and I see we've pulled up outside a *gelato* bar. He comes around to open the door for me and tells me my next clue is waiting inside—giving me no further clues.

Walking inside, I see the place is packed. Many Italians stand around the counter eating their gelato or drinking espresso. Through all the chaos of happy customers, a short Italian woman rushes up to me handing me another red envelope and a hazelnut *gelato* in a cup. She winks and then gets right back to work. She doesn't even say a word.

I take my ice cream and note outside.

Opening the envelope—

*Enjoy your favorite dessert my sweet! I wish I could be licking it off your gorgeous body—maybe that's what I'll do later. ;)*

*Go to the place where coins bring wishes.*

*Your love,*

*Leo*

Looking up at Mateo, who was waiting for me to finish reading the note, I say, "We need to go to the Trevi Fountain."

I'm disappointed I can only take a few bites of my gelato because my stomach is still in knots—like a million little butterflies dancing inside. I hate the thought of wasting something so delicious, but this must be a sign of how eager I truly am. I never turn down gelato.

We pull up outside the Trevi Fountain and I jump out of the town car like a kid on Christmas. I have no idea what I'm supposed to look for. I scan the people throwing coins over their shoulders and I have a sudden sense of déjà vu. Have I done this before? Must have been when I came to Italy when I was a teenager.

I'm staring around, looking at everything with a detective's eye, when a young boy and his mom walk up to me. The boy asks if I'm Elena, even though I can tell he knows exactly who I am. His mom smiles and urges him to hand me the red envelope he's holding. With trembling hands, I take the envelope and rip it open.

When I look back up I notice the mom and son are gone.

*I will **fight** to gain back your trust.*
*I will **conquer** your heart & make you mine.*
*I will **win** your love.*
*We are **champions** when we are together.*

Fight ... conquer ... win... champions.

"Mateo! We need to go to the Colosseum." I rush back toward the car.

"Wait!" He hands me a coin. "You need to make a wish at the fountain. Why waste the trip?"

I really don't want to waste time getting to the Colosseum, but Mateo looks interested in this game. Okay, I'll throw the stinkin' coin into the famous fountain. I swear this is super silly, but after all Mateo's done for him, I'll do it.

Positing myself with my back to the fountain, I think hard about my wish. I decide I'll wish for my memories of Leo back—yes, even the not-so-good ones—I want them all.

I throw the coin over my shoulder and think—

*I wish for true unconditional love and a happy marriage!*

74

Where did that come from? That's not the wish I was planning to make and it completely catches me off guard.

But it feels right, like it's meant to be. Do I even want the things I just said? Well, yes, of course. Will Leo provide those things? I have no clue and I'll never know if I stand at this fountain forever.

Mateo stops the car outside the Colosseum, near a private entrance away from the long line of tourists waiting to get inside. I'm escorted inside by a staff member and taken to a great view of the interior arena. I stand at the railing and look out at the enormous space and imagine what it would look like full of people.

Terrifying yet thrilling. A piece of history.

As I'm looking out, I don't even bother to look for a clue as I figure someone will come up to me and, just like the past two locations, I'm correct. An older man with a cane walks up to me with a red envelope.

"You're just as lovely in person," he says and hands me the envelope.

I can barely say thank you before he darts away.

*There's no clue for your last spot. Mateo knows where to go.*

*If you're ready to give me another try to win your heart, let him know you want to go to the next destination.*

*If not & your fresh start still stands, I can't bear the thought of me without you. You are my love.*

*And I can promise you I've never said that to another woman, ever. I've never felt this for another woman, ever.*

*There is no one else for me.*

*Your Leo*

## 11

Reading the last letter a good five more times, I leave the Colosseum in search of Mateo. He's standing nearby, of course, never taking me out of his sight. He gives me a questioning look but doesn't say anything to pressure me either way.

Getting into the town car, I read the letter one more time for good measure.

*You are my love.*

*There is no one else for me.*

Isn't this just what I threw a stupid coin into a fountain and wished for? A love like this. Maybe there was a reason I lost my memories. At first I was throwing myself a pity party over having my memories gone, and then I was angry everyone knew the details about my life than me. From there I launched into this charade of starting fresh.

Has leading up to this moment been my fate all along?

To wipe the drama with Leo away for a new beginning. To give him the chance to prove himself. For me to see what I fought for—what I was willing to give my life for.

"Take me to Leo," I say to Mateo, who was patiently waiting for my answer.

"As you wish. You've made a good choice."

"What were you instructed to do if I said to take me home?"

I know Leo would have a plan for anything.

"To drive around the city for hours until you changed your mind."

I knew it! He's relentless. I laugh at what a crazy man he is, and Mateo laughs too.

"Mateo, I feel like over this time you've been my bodyguard, you've gotten to know me better as a person."

"Of course, *Signora* Scott. I have the utmost respect for you."

"With that respect in mind, could you answer a question for me? Do you think Leo is a good choice for me? I decided I can't judge him for his past mistakes if I can't remember them, but I don't want to be made a fool again. What do you think?"

Mateo takes a minute to compose his answer and then he breathes deeply.

"I've known *Signor* Forte since he was a little boy—maybe two or three years old. Always running around, getting into things he shouldn't have, exploring, and asking questions. Doing what little boys do.

"Even though he was a little boy, he had the heart of a giant. Always kind—toward family, strangers, animals, other kids—he wanted to give everything that he owned to them." Mateo pauses for a moment to take a sharp right turn, never taking his eyes off the road as he speaks. "Then his father passed away and his mother closed herself off to the world. I saw a shift in Leonardo. He'd never admit it but he closed himself off too. He threw himself into his schooling then work—I think making up for the fact that he was now the man of his family. A family watched by the public eye.

"He took me on as his private staff and I've been by his side every step of the way. I've seen everything—including his lack of real relationships with women. Yes, he'd take women on dates but he'd cycle through them like they meant nothing. Before you, I can honestly say I've never seen him open his heart toward anyone like this.

"I don't think he'd tell you this but he hadn't gone into a hospital since his father passed. Even with his mother's breast cancer scare, he'd be waiting for her at home after each test. He can't stand being in a hospital. But when you were shot, he stayed there every single day.

He never went home. He stood by your side willing you to get better, to wake up."

He stops the car in front of a restaurant, which I recognize was directly across the street from the Colosseum. Mateo drove around in circles to answer my question. And what an answer it was.

"Mateo, *grazie* for your honesty."

He takes my hand and leads me toward the front door of the restaurant.

From there a waitress escorts me up several flights of stairs to a rooftop patio as the day has grown into early evening, and the sun's oranges and reds light the sky with the Colosseum directly across the street.

My Mr. Beautiful waits for me, standing at our table. Looking around, I notice it's the only table on this rooftop patio—we have the place to ourselves.

Red rose petals and candles trail the way to the table. My heart melts. No one has ever done anything this romantic for me before, ever.

I walk slowly toward Mr. Beautiful and he flashes his perfect white teeth at me in a captivating smile.

"*Cara,* I'm glad you've decided to join me." I don't know if he's surprised or not, he's not giving anything away.

"Leo, I don't know what this means for us, but I know that I love having you in my life."

He pulls the chair out for me and then pours both of us flutes of champagne. Rose petals frozen inside ice cubes are in the champagne bucket.

"Your scavenger hunt was a lot of fun. Who were all those people with the envelopes?"

"I've never done anything like that before," he says, taking a sip of his champagne. "Those were employees at Forte Enterprises—except for the lady in the gelato bar. She's the owner and a friend. They were all very excited to help me out and to get a glimpse of the woman who stole my heart."

"I bet! I was so excited I couldn't even eat my *gelato.*"

"I'll take you back one day for more," he promises with a laugh.

Our waiter approaches with an appetizer of prosciutto cups, and Leo lets me know that he's taken the liberty to order for us. I've secretly always wanted a man who takes charge of any situation. It's exhausting always being the one who makes the decisions. I'm also used to always picking up the bill for my ex-boyfriends and me. #IDontWantNoScrubs

I dig into the appetizer and let out a little moan of pleasure.

Wiping my mouth with the cloth napkin, I place it back into my lap and look up to find Leo's eyes transfixed on me. He hasn't touched his food. His eyes look dark and he looks hungry for one thing and one thing only: me.

"I could watch you eat for days," he says, reaching for his own food. "I've told you this before. You make the cutest little noises when you eat something you enjoy. I think I'm hard now, just from hearing you." He laughs.

Before I can allow him to turn yet another conversation sexual, there's been something on my mind I'm dying to know.

"Have you been with anyone since I ended things between us?" I blurt out.

I'm nervous to hear his answer, but I need to know, especially after deciding to show up here when he made an ultimatum.

"No—you're it for me."

Just like that, I let go of the breath I didn't even realize I was holding. He had absolutely no reason to wait for me to come around—because I didn't even know myself if I was going to—it makes me feel much better to hear no other woman has been with him.

"Can you say the same?" He cocks an eyebrow.

"No," I utter, intoxicated by his eyes on me, "I mean ... yes! I can say the same, I haven't been with anyone else. I did kiss my neighbor—but kissing was as far as we went."

Leo laughs a belly laugh. "Are you trying to give me a heart attack, *bella?*"

"I'm sorry! I was happy to hear you haven't slept with anyone else that I wasn't really paying attention to your question," I say.

"I don't think I could ever sleep with anyone else ever again. You and I have something electric. You might not remember, but our sex was always very passionate. You've ruined me for all other women."

"That makes me nervous."

"Why?"

"Because ... what if I don't remember how to be *that* girl? I don't think I've ever had passionate sex with anyone before. I can say my past boyfriends weren't complimenting me on my sex appeal."

Leaning back from the table, I fold my arms across my chest, letting my insecurities creep over me.

"I will gladly throw all this food off the table and fuck you right here, right now. I'd be happy to put my tongue between your thighs and make *you* my dinner. Your gorgeous tits for my appetizer and your pussy for my main course. I can assure you that you have sex appeal. Don't ever doubt yourself again."

Another pair of panties drenched by Leo.

*I sure hope I don't let him down!*

His hand is on top of the table and I reach over to interlock our fingers. Contemplating what Mateo told me in the car about Leo being in a hospital for the first time since his father's death just to be with me. There's also the fact that he's put up with my confusion and mood swings. Not to mention me shoving him out of my life.

But he's here—willing to try again.

I take a deep breath and then pour out my feelings.

"Thank you for having confidence in me. Thank you for waiting for me. Thank you for staying in the hospital with me. Thank you for being kind to me even though I feel like I've been a crazy woman. Thank you for putting this date together. Thank you for ... *everything.*"

I squeeze his hand, wishing in this moment he would make good on his threat—throwing all this food off the table and fucking me on top of it. I want him all over me, inside of me.

"You don't have to thank me for anything. Not a single thing. You did the most selfless thing anyone could ever do for another person by jumping in front of that bullet. I owe you thanks."

"I understand why I took that bullet for you," I say with 100-percent certainty. "Now I wish I could remember who fired it."

Our waiter strolls back to our table carrying a big tray of food—
two juicy T-bone steaks, sautéed spinach, and more champagne.

We eat and talk, answering some of the basic 'getting to know you
more' questions as we watch the sunset over the Eternal City sky.

As fun as this date is, I'm ready to get out of here and get myself
beneath this man. If I don't have his cock inside me tonight, I'll
scream. Actually, let's hope I am screaming.

———

Mateo drives us back to Leo's home in Tivoli, just outside of Rome,
and surprisingly other than cuddling we keep our hands to ourselves on
the whole ride, sadly for my needy self.

I wouldn't mind a quick fuck in the back of that town car.

*You're such a dude; he probably wants to make your new 'first time' some-
thing special.*

We curl up together with wine glasses and a blanket on his couch in
front of a cozy warm fire.

"Can you share a happy memory between us with me?" I ask Leo,
nuzzling in a little closer. He smells divine. If we could bottle up his
scent and sell it, we'd make a fortune.

"Let's see ... the first time we had sex was right over there," he says,
pointing toward a brown bearskin rug in front of the fire.

I study the rug like it's going to come to life. I've been here before,
in front of this fire, and I'm not mad that I don't remember. Instead,
I'm excited to create a new memory in its place—for both Leo and me.

"Do you see that happening again tonight?" I run my hand down
his chest, reaching for the buttons on his shirt. He grabs my small
hand in his large one to stop me.

"No."

*"No?"* I repeat the word back like it's poison on my tongue.

*I swore I wasn't making up his attraction to me. Why is he stopping?*

"Not here."

He sits our wine glasses on the marble cocktail table in front of the
couch, throws the blanket off of us, and scoops me up into his arms—
all without saying another word.

Wrapping my arms around his tan neck, he carries me up a flight of stairs toward what I'm hoping is his bedroom.

Leo kicks the door open and I'm in a gothic yet romantic bedroom —with a king mahogany bed covered with red sheets. He turns on a dim light, setting the mood.

Placing me down, I stand with my feet on the floor. This is really happening.

Reaching out a trembling hand, I reattempt my mission to strip him. He lets me slowly undo each button and slide the dress shirt to the floor. I run my fingers along this muscular chest and feel the heat of his skin against my own.

When I reach for his belt, he stops me. He wraps his hand around my long ponytail and pulls hard. I let out a moan, realizing when he's a little rough with me I get wet. His sinful mouth claims mine and his tongue thrusts inside. With sweeping strokes I meet his tongue with my own. Every muscle in my body quivers—with just a kiss I'm coming undone.

"I want you to sit on my face," he growls at me, his eyes dark with lust.

My breath catches in my chest. "I've never done that before," I whisper. No one has ever asked me to do this and I've never asked a man to let me. I've never been comfortable enough with my own body or sexuality.

*But riding Leo's face sounds so fun.*

Shut up inner bitch, you are dirty.

He smirks. "You'll do great, *bella*. I want you to have this experience, it's for *your* pleasure."

Without saying a word, I let my guard down for him. I trust him. I keep my eyes glued to his, as I reach around my skirt and unzip it. Slowly sliding it down my legs, I step out and leave it behind on the marble floor along with his dress shirt. I shimmy down my panties and toss them toward his chest.

Leo catches my pink panties and twirls them around his finger. His playfulness cracks me up and calms my nerves.

"Are you going to lay down?" I ask.

He smiles and then lies down on the bed. Climbing up on top of his firm body, I straddle his chest. I put my hands down and stroke through his light chest hair.

"You're going to have to sit a little higher up, *bella.*" He teases.

I know exactly where I need to sit, but I need a second to gain my composure and then continue to move up his body toward his luscious mouth.

My pussy is directly over his face now, spread wide, as I grab on to the headboard facing the wall.

Before I can have second thoughts, a long glorious stroke of his tongue sends electricity to my core. He stops at my clit and sucks it between his lips. Gripping onto the headboard for dear life, a low moan escapes from the back of my throat.

"You taste delicious." Leo quickly flicks his tongue back and forth over my throbbing nub. My pussy clenches and a pull starts to form in my stomach, desperate for him to go faster.

I'm completely overtaken in this moment. Rocking my hips, I grind over his expert tongue. As I grind on his face, he drives his tongue inside my entrance. The stubble from his slight beard rubs me in just the right places on my thighs.

Now this is where I'd normally pull back, close down emotionally and fake an orgasm just to get it over with. Knowing that no boyfriend has ever taken me all the way.

*Give yourself to him.*

"Don't stop!" I plead, holding myself steady over him now.

I could easily collapse from the pressure that's building up inside of me. He aggressively grabs my ass cheeks and thrusts my sex hard right against his warm mouth. I almost lose my grip on the headboard, caught in surprise.

Leo sucks hard and I lose my mind. Closing my eyes, I see an explosion of colors. When my out-of-body experience cools down enough for me to open my eyes again, I climb off Leo's gorgeous face and lay down next to him. My legs still tremble down to my toes.

*I've never had an orgasm like that ... that I can remember.*

"Was that as good for you as it was for me?" he asks me with a devilish grin as he wipes my juices off his handsome face.

"It was ... alright," I joke as I turn the tables and reach for his zipper.

This time he doesn't stop me. Before I pull down his pants, I plant a kiss on his lips—showing him appreciation for what he's just done for me. His pants are off and in a matter of seconds I have his thick, swollen manhood between my hands.

"Let me show you just how 'alright' that was for me," I say before flicking my tongue across the tip of his cock, swiping off a lick of juices. His mouth falls open and I hear a moan escape before he grips onto my ponytail again.

Curling my tongue from the tip of his large cock to his balls where I gently massage his balls, before putting one in my mouth and sucking.

"Fuck," Leo cries out, giving me just the encouragement I need to keep going.

With long strokes of my tongue I get his dick drenched before putting it into my warm mouth as far as I can possibly take him. I bob my mouth up and down on his cock, swirling my tongue around before sucking on his tip. I add my hands to pump him at the same time.

"Stop, Elena. Fuck ... I want to come inside of you," Leo says.

Leo pulls my ponytail hard enough that my mouth loses contact with its favorite toy. He pulls my body up away from his cock, and now I'm laying beneath him as he plants a string of warm kisses from my earlobe down my neck.

He cups my breast and latches on to my right nipple with his mouth. It instantly hardens for him, and I moan in ecstasy. I run my fingers through his thick hair as he moves his attention to my left nipple, giving it the same love he did the right. Pure bliss.

"Leo, I'm so close again," I pant out, as I grind my sex up to his body.

Leo positions himself above me and rubs his cock up and down my wet pussy. Our juices make his grinding so slick. Each time his tip grazes my clit, it takes me closer and closer to the edge again. Grinding my hips up to press further into him, I hope he takes the hint that I can't wait much longer.

Just when I think he's going to thrust himself inside of me, he pinches my clit between his fingers.

"Stop teasing me and take me ... now," I command.

"Someone is being a bit bossy, *bella*," he whispers in my ear before sucking on it. My body tingles with pleasure. "I'll give you what you want, don't worry."

Just then his cock finds my entrance and slowly slips its way inside —inch by inch. Sinking my nails into his biceps, I push him harder into me. I don't want it slow and sweet.

"Harder ... faster ... please, Leo."

He stops with the teasing, pulls his cock out, and then slams back into me. This time with the force I was looking for. I feel completely full. I have no idea what he hits inside my body, but whatever it is it's amazing.

Leo pulls himself completely out, making me feel empty inside. But before I can beg he pounds into me again. I grind my hips in sync with him and our bodies take over—moving as one.

We grind, thrust, and slam into each other over and over until we are both covered in sweat. I'm holding on to him for dear life, my nails digging into his back.

"Elena, come when I say," Leo commands.

I don't know if that will be possible, but I shut my brain off and just feel. I feel everything—I'm hypersensitive to each touch.

"Elena, now."

And together we reach our bliss as one. I throw my head back into the pillow and scream out, while continuing to pull his body down into mine with my arms wrapped around his back. I know he's just as affected as me—I hear him breathing heavily into my ear as he pulls his cock out.

"Oh my god. I think that was the most amazing thing I've ever experienced in my life," I say, squeezing his body a little tighter.

He's crushing my lungs, but I don't care. I don't want to let him go.

"I'm glad that was 'alright' for you." He laughs and positions himself so I can see his face. "I know you may not feel this yet and I understand, but I need you to know that ... I love you."

I don't care that this new 'no memories Elena' doesn't know

anything about her life, but something deep inside of me feels like this is right. My fate. I've never been so sure of anything before, ever. Not even million-dollar business deals that I didn't even blink an eye at.

"I love you too," I say before nibbling on his bottom lip.

"If you keep that up I'm going to be ready to go again."

*He can't be serious?* And before I can ask him if that's a joke, I feel Mr. Beautiful's cock spring back to life.

Bring on round two!

## 12

---

Waking up with a soreness between my thighs reminds me of the glorious night before. During round one ... two ... three ... or four.

*Four times!*

I can't remember the last time I wanted to have sex twice in one night with my past boyfriends. Hell no, that was a chore, but with Leo it's like a drug.

*Hello my name is Elena, and I'm addicted to sex with Leo.*

I crave him and can't get enough. Whatever he'll give, I'll happily take.

The sunlight streams across Leo's face and he looks so relaxed as he snores gently. He's not staring at me with heated eyes of desire or being so serious all the time. Just a man in his bed next to his woman sleeping peacefully. I love this moment.

Taking a second, I admire his features: his strong jawline, olive skin, and full black eyelashes that match his thick dark hair.

"If you keep staring at me like you're hungry, I'm going to give you something to eat," he growls without even opening his eyes.

"Well, damn! I didn't think you could possibly think about that right now, after all we did last night." I blush knowing he caught me gawking over him when I thought he was still asleep.

He opens his emerald eyes and smiles before rolling over to prop himself up on his elbow—mirroring my pose.

"I will *always* be ready for you," he says before taking his other hand and skimming it down the red sheet to rub over my nipple. "But I think Gemma is downstairs with our breakfast waiting, and I'd love to let her wait because you are more important, but I do have a few things to discuss with her before she leaves."

For a second, I freak out at the mention of another woman's name, but I remember he told me about his connection to his close staff members— Gemma and Mateo—when he was helping me to get my memories back. They've both been in his life since he was a little boy. They're all devoted to one another, which makes me happy to know he has such caring people in his life.

But wait—what about that mother who doesn't like me? Where has she been?

Before I can ask my question, Leo claims my mouth with his.

"What was that for?" I squeak out.

"It looked like you were overthinking about something unpleasant and I wanted it to stop."

"I was actually thinking about your mother," I spit out.

"Right now?" He lifts the sheets to reveal our naked bodies. "This is the time you want to think about my mother." He wrinkles his nose. "What about her?"

I laugh. "I haven't heard anything about her since the shooting. And Sophie let me know that she doesn't like me."

"I think I should have a talk with Sophie myself."

*Oops! I didn't mean to throw my best friend under the bus like that.*

"Are you okay with having a relationship with someone who your family doesn't like?"

"Elena, I don't give a shit what my mama has to say," he states as he cups my chin lifting my eyes to meet his. "You haven't heard about her since the shooting because I haven't really spoken with her. After it happened, I was very angry with her and shut her out. She's been able to ... how you Americans say 'weasel' her way back into my life because we work in some of the same charity circles ... but that's it."

"You don't have to end your relationship with her because of me. I think family is so important—I would do anything for mine."

"And I love that about you," he says before kissing my cheek. "I would, of course, do anything to help her if she needs me, but when it comes to us, she can't control my heart or who I give it to. I'll fight for you Elena, until my heart stops beating."

Leaning in, I kiss his cheek, so touched by what he's said. It takes a special kind of person to stand up to their family for someone they are in a relationship with. I don't think any of my past boyfriends would have done this, and to be honest I don't think I would have fought for any of them either.

"Alright, enough overthinking. As much as I hate seeing you put on your clothes, I think it's time we head downstairs," he says before sliding out of the bed to put on his gray sweat pants. I catch a glimpse of his ridiculously toned ass, and I fight the urge to take a bite out of it. He turns around to spot me staring yet again and I bust out laughing.

"Okay, you caught me! I was admiring that hot ass of yours," I say before putting on my yoga pants and T-shirt.

"I've got a great view too, *bella*."

———

We walk downstairs to the kitchen hand-in-hand. Gemma has our plates set at the outdoor table on the patio. Yellow daisies fill a vase in the center of the table along with two cups of espresso as a short redhead Italian woman wanders out of the kitchen carrying two plates of French toast and bacon

"*Bon appetito!*" she says before excusing herself back into the house.

The food smells marvelous, and in my first bite I find a surprise: the French toast is stuffed with a rich cream cheese. I must have let out one of those little moans of joy because when I look up Leo has his eyes on mine.

"Did I do it again?"

He leans in and wipes his finger across my lips, catching some cream cheese that must have gotten on my face, and then he sticks his finger out toward me. I pull his finger into my mouth and suck the cream cheese off. Slowly.

"Well isn't that something I'd rather not see so early in the morning," says a matter-of-fact Italian voice from the patio doors.

I turn around in my chair to find a short woman with short brown hair and green eyes to match Leo's. This must be—

"Mama, what are you doing here? Especially unannounced," Leo says, wiping his fingers in a white cloth napkin.

*Fingers I just had in my mouth in front of his mom!*

"Well son, I see your manners toward me haven't gotten any better, even with your little girlfriend back," Rosalie says as she takes a seat at the table across from me and next to Leo. "Are you doing okay Elena? I'm sorry to hear about that ridiculous shooting."

*Ridiculous?*

That's not a word I'd use to describe what happened to us.

Horrific.

Life threatening.

Chilling.

Yes. But ridiculous? That's a word I'd use to describe a clown or comedy show.

"Yes, I'm doing much better. Thank you for asking." Maybe it's a good sign that she's asked about my health in general?

"Now that we've gotten that out of the way," she says turning her chair to face Leo completely, "Leonardo I'd like to talk to you about the charity luncheon you've so graciously offered to host here this week. I've drawn up all the plans—seating, menu, invitations, media press release, and I wrote you a speech."

Leo grips his napkin a little too tightly and a vein in his neck bulges. Under the tablecloth, I slip my hand into his and gently squeeze it. His expression softens.

"I told you that you could have your luncheon here, but I didn't say that I wanted to be involved in any part of it." Leo drops the poor napkin that he had trapped in a death grip. "You know I don't want to, nor do I have the time for this. I was going to talk to Gemma this morning to put her in charge of the menu and setup—you can show her your plans," he says nodding toward her big stack of papers. "As for the press release, you can send it to Natalia to take care of. And there will be no speech from me."

"It upsets me how cold you can be toward your own mother," she says. She turns to me now and says, "I've heard that you don't have any memories of being in Italy. Which is a pity. But I want to remind you that I don't think you are good enough for my son and you are the reason our relationship is suffering."

I can't believe she just said that to my face.

"That's enough!" Leo slams his fist down on the table, causing everything to shake.

His mother looks startled by Leo's violence and she immediately pushes her chair out from the table, clutching her papers to her chest.

"That's enough? I will not let you speak to me like this or act like some caveman. I will see myself out and I will see you at that luncheon," Rosalie says before heading back toward the patio doors and leaving.

Leo has his fist still clenched on top of the table and he's looking down at his mostly untouched food.

Pushing my chair back, I surprise him by cuddling into his lap. I wrap my arms around his neck, and he wraps his around my body.

He meets my eyes and softly says, "I'm so sorry for what just happened. I want you to know that I don't agree with anything she says. Those are not my thoughts."

"Hey," I say, taking one hand to cup his cheek, "it's okay, baby. You are not responsible for your mom's actions—or anyone else's actions for that matter. And you stood up for me, that meant a lot." I lean in to kiss his delectable lips. "So tell me about this charity luncheon that's going to be taking place here?"

"Ugh. I completely forgot about it because I've been wrapped up in much better things," he says before trailing kisses down my neck, "but my mama called a few days ago to force her way into letting her host the event here. She has a mansion and still she wants to use mine. I think it's because she rarely opens her world up to people. No one is welcome in her home. And I also think she wants to trap me into being involved in her work."

"Is there anything I can do to help out?"

Leo looks at me like I've said something crazy. "Why would you want to help her? She treats you badly. I'd think you'd want nothing to do with her. And I wouldn't blame you for thinking that."

I look sincerely into his eyes. "She's your mother and even though she's mean to me, she's doing something to help other people through charity. I can admire that. My company frequently donates money and time to local charities in Michigan—we just want to make a difference. Why not do the same in my new home?"

"Elena, you're an amazing woman."

If only his mother shared the same sentiment.

## 13

My shift—an eventful one at that—is finally ending for the day. We hired Josephina, a new employee studying business in college, and I am the one in charge of training her. She's incredibly sweet. I can't believe I was able to convince Marco to hire more help—for so long it's just been me and him, or so I've been told.

The coffee shop is booming with business; we've done two more poetry nights, and we are now advertising our business on social media and through Yelp. I hope Stella would be proud of all that we are doing to turn her business around and get Marco out of this massive debt she's left behind.

On the walk toward my apartment, I take a detour and look at all the sights and sounds of Rome. Walking past children running through the streets kicking soccer balls makes me smile. There are also markets of fresh fruits and vegetables, other caffés and bars with patios outside full of people drinking coffees and eating sandwiches. Smiling faces and happiness all around.

Has it always been like this?

*You're in love and seeing things in a new light!*

Can that be true?

True or not, I walk and walk and walk until I look up to see a tall building, "Forte Enterprises." As much as I used to hate interruptions in the office, I decide I'm going to surprise my man.

Pulling open the double glass doors, I walk toward a younger looking secretary with a cute brunette Pixie cut sitting behind a huge glass desk. She has a headset on and she's talking a million miles per minute. Men and women in stylish business suits walk through the lobby carrying briefcases. Everyone looks in a hurry, which is surprising for Italians. I hear chatter of projects, proposals, and deadlines.

I must look completely out of place in my Stella's white T-shirt and black skirt—but no one seems to stare at me. They actually all look right past me. What's funny is that this corporate world is my element. My office in Michigan has a similar hustle and bustle, however, there's no dress code.

Everyone is free to express himself or herself in any way. If you can create a killer Facebook ad campaign for a multi-million dollar company wearing jeans, then go for it. Just get the job done.

As I'm daydreaming about my office back home, the secretary stops talking for a brief second to address me.

"I don't think we ordered any more baked goods today." That's all she says before returning to her computer.

*What was that about?*

"Well that's good because I didn't bring any baked goods." I laugh as she continues ignoring me for her computer screen. "I'm here to see Leonardo Forte."

"He's not expecting anyone today," she says without even looking up.

"He's not, but I don't think he'd mind. If you could just tell me how to get to his office."

"Listen, a lot of people come here trying to talk to *Signor* Forte and he doesn't have time for that. If you want me to leave him your phone number, I can give it to him," she says now looking me up and down, "but I doubt he'll have time to call you back."

As I'm about to jump across this desk to bitch smack this woman for trying to keep me away from Leo, Mateo shows up next to me. Why do I forget he's always around?

"Angelina, *Signor* Forte will be very upset if you turn *Signora* Scott away. I would put her on the list of visitors who should *always* be allowed instant access to him," Mateo says.

He means business. If he wasn't my bodyguard, I would be a little scared of him right now.

"*Signor* Colonna, I didn't know she was someone important. I'm very sorry," Angelina says before quickly turning back toward me. "*Signor* Forte is on the twenty-third floor, you'll see his assistant Natalia's desk when you exit the elevator. I'll let her know you are on your way up. This won't happen again," she assures me.

Looks like Angelina knows when to back down. I turn toward Mateo and realize I just learned his last name. How could I not know the last name of the guy following me around all hours of the day?

"*Grazie* Mateo!"

I jump into the elevator with Mateo.

"Why didn't you jump in sooner and save me from the wrath of Angelina?"

Mateo laughs. "I wanted to see how that conversation would play out. I was hoping you'd put her in her place. Someone needed too."

I laugh. The elevator doors open to floor 23. Just like Angelina said, I find a woman whom I'm guessing is Natalia sitting at a marble desk outside of double doors.

"*Signora* Scott?" Natalia says in a much calmer demeanor than Angelina's. "*Signor* Colonna, lovely to see you again." Her smile looks friendly and she tells me Leo is on a conference call but she will buzz me through into his office.

I ask her if he's gotten word that I'm here and she assures me he hasn't—my surprise is still a surprise.

I hear a buzz and Natalia nods toward the double doors. I pull one and quietly make my way into the biggest office I've ever seen with floor-to-ceiling windows along a back wall overlooking downtown Rome. This time I leave Mateo outside.

Leo's back is toward the door, and I hear him talking to several voices coming through a speakerphone on his desk.

*Let's make this surprise visit worthwhile.*

Taking my Stella's white T-shirt off, I also slip my black skirt and shoes off. I silently walk toward his chair. Leo doesn't look up until I'm standing directly in front of him in just a pair of purple silk undies and a purple push-up bra to match. Everything on display for him.

"Fuck, Elena," Leo says in a deep voice.

"Excuse me, *signor?*" Someone on the conference line asks.

Putting my finger to my lips, I motion for him to "ssh" as I get down on my knees in front of him. The man normally always in control looks completely caught off guard.

I reach for his black belt and he grabs my hand to stop me but I wave him off. I remove off his belt, placing it behind me on the floor, and then pull down his dress pants and boxer briefs.

He's hard already, which makes me happy.

Leaning forward, I lick his cock like I've been hungry for it all day. Up and down I lick, stopping to suck on each ball, before taking him as far into my mouth as I possibly can. I hear him breathe out a sigh as he continues talking to his business associates.

*How is he remaining so composed? Let's change that!*

Leo takes his hand and pulls my hair up to hold on to. He uses my hair to push and pull my mouth up and down to fuck his cock. I'm taking him deeper and deeper with my mouth as he guides me, while my hand massages his balls. I gag loudly as I've got his entire cock touching the back of my throat. I don't think I've ever taken anyone this deep.

Someone on his conference lines asks if anyone heard that weird sound, worrying that their line isn't secure. I laugh a little on the inside knowing these high-powered business men and women are worrying about secure phone lines when I'm sucking my man off in his office.

Leo leans forward to unclasp my bra and I shimmy out of it before he cups my breast in his warm hand. He massages it aggressively while I take his cock back into my eager-to-please mouth. Pumping him with my hand like my life depends on it, I swirl my tongue around his cock. He tries to suppress little growls as he answers a question from an associate.

I take my mouth off his cock and flick my tongue over and over across the tip—getting it as wet as I can. I look up at him knowing he's

96

got to be close to having an orgasm. He squeezes my breast and rolls my nipple between his fingers.

I take Leo back deep into my mouth and he instantly lets go of my breast and tilts his head back, eyes closed, and lets out the most passionate sounding growl I've ever heard as he explodes inside my mouth. My panties are wet. I'm so turned on by pleasing him, but I didn't come here for me. I reach over for my bra but Leo grabs my hand and shakes his head 'no' at me.

"I'm sorry to cut this call short but it looks like an emergency has come up in my office. Something very important I need to take care of. You can continue to talk, email me the bullet points when you've finished," Leo says to his partners.

After the line clicks off, he practically leaps out of his chair, pushing me back onto the floor with his large body on top of mine. He takes the breast he's been teasing into his mouth and sucks as hard as he can on my tender nipple. I arch my back, loving this sensation.

There are three loud knocks on his door.

"What the fuck?" Leo whispers with a look of irritation on his handsome face.

"*Signor* Forte, Giorgio is out here ready for your 4:30 appointment," Natalia says through the intercom.

"Tell him I need a few minutes," he says. "Damn it! She's right, I do have an appointment that I need to take," Leo says, still on top of me. I run my fingers through his thick hair and claim his mouth with my own.

"It's okay, I dropped in on you unexpectedly. You can't change your whole day around for me. I know what it's like to run a big office too."

"I love that you understand, and I want to one day see your office. You know I'd cancel this appointment in a heartbeat but everything got turned around with the," he pauses for a moment looking depressed, "shooting."

He put his whole life on hold for me once already and it melts my heart. I press another deep kiss to his lips and crawl out from under him to get dressed.

"It was my pleasure to service you, Mr. Forte," I grin at him before I plant another kiss on him—this time on his cheek.

He catches my face between both hands and gives me the biggest smile I've ever seen.

"Did I say something funny?"

"No," he returns a kiss to my cheek, "but you have said something sassy like that to me before."

*I did? What was I doing to service him then?* I'm jealous of whatever it was.

"Have I done this before ... in your office?" I'm jealous of that thought too.

"*This?* You mean ... let me fuck your beautiful mouth?" Now look who's being sassy.

"Yes, that ... mouth fucking."

"I never kiss and tell, Elena," he says before smacking my ass as I head toward the double doors to leave. "I'll call you tonight."

Walking out into the lobby, I see another businessman with dark brown hair and eyes blue as the sky. This must be Giorgio. He looks up at me with a smile. I'm now familiar with this type of smile—we have met before.

"Elena! So nice to see you again. I'm sorry to hear about the shooting and your injuries. I surely hope the police are doing all they can to catch this crazy man," he says with a thick Italian accent.

*This man?*

Did anyone say the shooter was a man before? I don't remember anything from that day. Police are taking leads on both genders.

I must be staring at hime with a blank expression on my face because he quickly turns to Natalia and asks a few questions in Italian —I don't catch what he's saying because my mind is spinning.

I quickly say a goodbye and walk away from them both. I stop around the corner before entering the elevator to catch my breath. Something feels wrong. I turn back to walk toward Leo's office when I hear Giorgio talking in a hushed whisper to Natalia, his body language screaming anger.

"Wasn't she just the rudest person? She didn't even answer my question." I can't hear Natalia's reply but he continues, "Is this guy going to let me in yet? I've been waiting out here for 15 fucking minutes. Just because he's the boss doesn't mean we all don't have other shit to do. Entitled piece of shit asshole."

Well, that's not very nice.

Natalia tries to hush Giorgio down. She's even looking at him like he's crazy, but Leo suddenly opens the door to let his employee in. Giorgio quickly puts a smile on his face and stands up taller, releasing what looked like a posture of anger. He's transformed into a completely new person.

"*Signor* Forte, I'm excited to talk about the developments the research marketing team has made in the last month," Giorgio says happily as he walks toward Leo.

What the heck? That was weird. Very weird.

I make a mental note to talk to Leo about this later.

## 14

"Are you going to finish that?" Marco asks I put my half-eaten pork panini down.

"Not with you staring at it like you may actually rip my fingers off and finish it yourself," I say, passing the sandwich across the table toward him. "Be my guest, please."

I sip my espresso and open my laptop. Marco and I are officially having our first formal business meeting before the caffé opens in an hour. It's a Sunday and we open later for the church crowd.

It's also been three days since the 'mouth fucking' in Leo's office and I haven't seen him since. Not that I'm counting the days or anything. Okay, I'm totally counting and I miss my Mr. Beautiful. He's been swamped with work and I completely understand. I haven't had the chance to bring up the weird experience with Giorgio either because it feels strange to describe what I saw over a text message. Now that I've had time to think about it, anyone could get a little angry with his or her boss. Right?

"*Ciao* Elena, are you joining me for this meeting?" Marco asks, shoving my own damn sandwich in my face while laughing. *Why is every guy in my life so sassy?*

"Sorry for spacing out. Okay, let's talk about what we've been doing that's working really well in the last few months and what we should consider ditching or revamping."

I pull up a spreadsheet on my laptop and we get straight to business. We talk through all the revenue numbers since I've started and make a giant list of things we could revamp. We also pat ourselves on the back for turning around a lot of disastrous areas. According to Marco, his *nonna's* strengths were baking, making a mean cup of espresso, and building relationships with her loyal customers ... many who are still regulars today. Her weaknesses were tracking where her money went and paying bills on time ... or at all.

I'm closing my laptop and heading toward the back room to change into an apron—the irony of this situation does not escape me—when I hear a loud pounding on the front door. Our church regulars aren't usually the kind to beat the door down, so I wonder who could this be?

"Girl, I can see you! Open the door," Sophie shouts.

I run over to the door and open it, but I'm shocked she's standing here in front of me. I've known this girl since the seventh grade and she still surprises me with how stunning she is. I'd say she's a spitting image of Blake Lively—long blonde hair draping her shoulders with even longer legs to match. She pushes past me trailing two giant suitcases.

"What the heck are you doing here? Don't you have a company to run in Michigan?"

"Ha ha, Miss CEO who ran away. I came to check on you. What are best friends for?" Sophie says.

"Uh, Soph," I say pointing toward her suitcases, "you planning to move here too?"

"I wish! My boss is such a bitch, she would never let me leave my cage in Michigan," she says, laughing. "No, this suitcase is practically empty. I plan to buy shoes—and lots of them!"

"That's why I love you!"

We both laugh as Marco walks out from the back room and almost trips while carrying a huge tray of cannoli. I rush over to grab the tray and put them in the display case. It doesn't escape me that during this whole 'almost ruined all the baked goods' debacle, Sophie and Marco are awkwardly staring at each other, not saying a word.

"You guys forget your manners? I actually remember that you both already know each other—I know you were talking at the hospital," I say, hoping that pointing out the obvious will awaken my friends from their weird silence.

"Elena, I have something to tell you," Sophie says, turning toward me with a thoughtful look on her face.

"Okay." Now I'm a little nervous. Sophie has never needed to tell me something that required her serious voice. Actually I don't know if I've ever heard Sophie's serious voice before, ever.

Bitchy voice—check.

Loud voice—check.

Caring voice—check.

Loving voice—sometimes (check).

Business voice—check.

An "I have something to tell you" serious voice—nope.

"Marco and I have been talking to each other," Sophie spits out at me. She's looking down at the floor turning red. She's blushing? That's my signature move, not Sophie's.

"Talking as in...? Something you two clearly aren't doing standing in this caffé." I turn to look at Marco who looks down at the floor. What's their problem?

"Talking as in ... getting to know each other better. We've been texting, talking on the phone, and FaceTiming—really all you can do when you live across an ocean from each other.".

"Are you serious?"

"Please don't be mad! We didn't want you to think we snuck off behind your back to start a relationship when you were in the hospital. We feel terrible about that," she exclaims

"Mad? Are you kidding? I'm so happy for you guys!"

I look at both of my friends who quickly lift their heads in surprise. They look at me and smile, and then they look at each other. How cute are they.

"So you don't care?" Marco asks.

"Why would I care? You two are the best people I know. I'm ecstatic you've found each other. And I'm a little upset that I didn't think to set you up in the first place. Damn, where was my head?"

"Well you were busy recovering and all," Sophie says as she pulls me into a one-armed hug.

"Come over here you crazy Italian," I say extending my other arm toward Marco.

He rushes over and we stand there in a big group hug.

"Wait a second," I say pulling away from my friends, "does that mean you won't be spending every minute of your trip with me?"

Sophie's smile falls from her face. "I mean if you need me, I'll be there every minute, Elena, I promise."

"Get real! I'm so glad you have other plans. Not to be rude, but I have to see my man too."

We both laugh in confessing that bros are coming before hoes on this one trip. Marco stares at us like we are aliens, only making us laugh harder.

---

After what turned out to be an exhausting shift—we had non-stop customers from the minute we officially opened until we closed around 6 p.m.—I start the walk toward my apartment. My phone vibrates indicating a new text message.

*"Cara, I miss your gorgeous face + delicious pussy. I've asked Mateo to bring you over when I get out of work. Please come."*

*"Begging me to 'come' & I haven't even gotten there yet?"*

*"Your smart mouth better be ready for what I have to give."*

He makes my heart skip a beat with the promise of what's waiting for me when I get to his house. I wave to Mateo when I get to my apartment and send him a text saying I'll be ready to come down whenever Leo gives the word.

As I walk up the stairs toward my apartment, I run into Brian as he's locking his front door. He's carrying his camera in one hand and an energy drink in the other; he looks just as exhausted as I feel. Dark circles are under his eyes, and I guess he hasn't combed his wild brown hair in days.

"Elena, I haven't seen you in probably a whole week. I've missed you! How have you been?"

"I've been doing good. More importantly, how are you? How's work?" I remember that he just started his new photography job.

"Insane! I've been doing projects all over Italy—catching buses and trains to go from location to location. But I got some awesome photos of the Blue Grotto in Naples and the seaside villages in the Cinque Terre. Right now, I've got some fancy party to photograph; I decided to pick up some freelance work. I'd love to show you my photos sometime."

"That would be nice." I lie because I'm terrible at blowing people off. I wouldn't mind seeing his work to support him as a friend.

But that's it—we can just be friends.

My phone buzzes again and Leo's name is displayed on the screen, and both Brian and I notice it.

"Is he your boyfriend?" Brian asks in a monotone voice with his eyes still glued to my iPhone screen.

"He is," I say, locking the phone screen and deciding to come clean about my relationship with Leo. "I wasn't completely honest with you and for that I'm sorry. Leo and I were dating before the shooting. After I couldn't handle not knowing any of the memories we had together, and the ones I did learn from friends didn't sound all that great. I decided to take a break for my own sanity, but we have since reconnected and are back together."

"I appreciate you telling me that. A girl like you deserves someone really great in your life, and I hope this guy is that for you," he says before taking a sip of his energy drink, "and I hope this doesn't mean we can't see each other in the halls—especially if you decide to do it in your sleepwear again."

I laugh at his corny joke and blush at the memory. We say our goodbyes and I go back into my apartment to check my text from Leo letting me know he's on his way home. I quickly pack an overnight bag, remembering to include some sexy lingerie. I've got a few ideas to repay Leo for that fun scavenger hunt. #BoomChickaWowWow

# 15

"Alright Mateo, I'm all ready to go," I say, rushing down the steps toward the man who I am so grateful is my bodyguard.

But I quickly notice Mateo doesn't greet me with my usually, *"Signorina Scott"* and smile. Instead he's looking down the street with a face deep in thought. I don't even think he's realized I'm standing at the car door. I can surely open my own door, but I stand there watching Mateo look off down the road. I walk up to him and touch his arm gently. He breaks his serious face and looks at me with a hesitant smile.

*"Signorina* Scott, you look lovely this evening. *Signor* Forte is already at the house. I think the man has texted me five times asking if we've left yet," he says chuckling as he opens the back door for me to get into the town car.

Before Mateo has the chance to put up the divider to offer me privacy I ask, "Mateo, what were you looking at just now? You looked upset."

"Elena, I don't want to concern you over something that could easily be nothing." He starts the car and we head toward Leo's home.

"You don't have to tiptoe around me. Please tell me if you saw something that alarmed you," I beg.

I'm not a little girl, and I'd like to be in on what's going on in my own life.

"I thought I saw a man standing on the street just loitering for longer than necessary. He wasn't with anyone, just looking from his phone to the street over and over. He didn't go into any buildings—and this street is just homes and apartments. When he noticed I was staring at him, he turned around and briskly walked away."

"Did you recognize him?"

"No, he had a hood up on his sweatshirt. It was one of those sweatshirts with the sleeves cut off—like he was out running and stopped—which is what I originally thought. He kept looking down toward his phone; I couldn't see his face. I'm sorry."

I look at Mateo's concerned face in the rearview mirror.

"There's no need to apologize! He wasn't doing anything wrong. There's no reason to approach him or anything. But Mateo, I do want to ask you a question. Do you know anything about Leo's employee, Giorgio?"

"Giorgio Piccolo? I don't know him personally well, but I know he works in the research and marketing department of Forte Enterprises. He did an internship with Leo when he was in college and then Leo hired him after because he admired his work ethic. He's in his early thirties and works a lot. Why do you ask?"

"When I was at the office the other day, he rubbed me the wrong way."

"He touched you?" Mateo says with anger in his eyes—I can't help to laugh at my poor translation.

"No, no. That's an American expression for, 'he gave me the creeps.' He didn't actually rub me," I say.

I can't stop laughing now as Mateo's face turns red.

*Mi dispiace,*" he says, apologizing for his adorable mistake. "How did he give you the creeps?" Hearing him say 'creeps' in his Italian accent is almost as funny as the rubbing mistake.

I launch into my story about how Giorgio mentioned that the shooter was a man when we don't know if that's true. I also tell Mateo about how I overheard Giorgio blow up on Natalia talking shit about Leo and me.

107

Mateo lets me tell him the whole story without interruption, looking between the roads ahead and at me in the rearview mirror.

"I'm going to check on this, Elena. Thank you for telling me. Next time, don't wait a few days, immediately tell me if someone rubs you wrongly." This time he laughs at the expression as we pull up at Leo's gorgeous home.

From the first time I saw this place, I feel in love with it. I love this home much better than his Rome apartment. A huge wrought iron gate opens as we pull into the circular driveway. Everything is draped in purple Wisteria flowers and my eye always catches the water fountain covered in moss in the middle of the driveway.

I find my Mr. Beautiful sitting at the kitchen table with his laptop and a stack of papers in front of him. He's typing feverishly and addressing someone through a Bluetooth he's wearing, but when he sees me walk in the room he immediately tells whoever it is on the other end that he's got to go.

"Working late, *Signor* Forte?" I say, taking a seat on top of the kitchen table and pushing his papers aside.

"I'd like to work on something else now," he says, moving his chair to sit right between my legs.

I'm wearing a pair of tiny jean shorts. He picks up my right leg and slowly plants kisses all the way up toward my thigh. I close my eyes and lean back, enjoying the sensations.

We hear a cough and Mateo says, "Excuse me. I'm sorry to interrupt but *Signor* Forte I need a word with you if that's okay."

I blush knowing Mateo's caught me spread out on the table but he doesn't make eye contact, thank God.

*"Bella,* I'll be back shortly. I never leave my work unfinished," he says as he winks and leans in for a kiss before leaving the room.

I know Mateo is going to fill Leo in on the stranger outside my apartment and Giorgio. I wish I had a chance to tell Leo myself, but I'm glad to have someone who knows how to handle the situation. I feel safe with these men I've only known a short time.

———

It's taking Leo and Mateo a lot longer than I thought, so I get up and explore the house. I take the stairs to the basement and find a killer workout room—state of the art equipment, floor to ceiling mirrors, and yoga mats. There's also a steam room and a double-head rainforest shower. This floor is bigger than my entire apartment here in Italy.

Actually my apartment back in Michigan isn't all that grand either —I've been known to be a little cheap. I save, save, and save for a rainy day. Don't get me wrong, I drive a kickass Mercedes and have my fair share of Christian Louboutins—but outside of a few luxury items, most of my money sits in stocks and investment accounts. Not what you expect from a 25-year-old. #Boring

This is one of the reasons I'm shocked that I'm in Italy in the first place. Before this I can't remember the last time I took a vacation.

I notice another set of stairs leading deeper into the house and find myself in a chilly wine cellar. There are rows and rows of wine bottles — I feel drunk just looking at them. There's even an entrance to a sitting area, which must be the wine bar. I grab a bottle, not knowing if it's any good or if it's a bazillion dollars, but I take it back with me up the two flights of stairs. I'll buy him another one if this is a collector.

On the main floor of the house I've already been into the kitchen, patio, and living room featuring the seductive fireplace. This floor also has a den and a library. I'm ecstatic to see this library! It even has a ladder to the second story of books. I'm in heaven. This is my Belle from *Beauty & The Beast* moment. #FavoritePrinces

I pull myself away from the library because I want to finish my tour, but remind myself I'm going to come back to curl up with a book by yet another fireplace if Leo and Mateo aren't done soon.

A double set of marble staircases stands at the main entrance to the house, and I take one of them and find a row of guest bedrooms to the left—everything is professionally decorated—and Leo's bedroom to the right, along with his office. The door to Leo's office is shut and I know that he and Mateo are on the other side talking about our safety. I want to barge in to hear what's going on but I decide to leave them be. I dash back downstairs to grab my overnight bag and find Gemma in the kitchen cleaning up Leo's stacks of messy papers.

"*Ciao* Elena, would you like something for dinner? And would you like me to open that bottle for you?" she nods at the white wine bottle in my hand.

I know there's an unspoken rule to never turn down an Italian woman's offer for food, so I accept. The same goes for the offer to open the wine.

I sit at the table that's now clear of Leo's mess and Gemma puts a basket of fresh bread and a plate with olive oil and roasted pine nuts in front of me, as well as a plate with a huge salad with dark, leafy greens and baked salmon.

I hope Leo knows I'll never be able to cook like this for him. Unless I took lessons or something. Maybe Gemma would teach me?

*Where did that thought come from?*

I've never considered learning how to cook for someone else. I take pride in the fact that I will not be anything like a 'housewife' for any man, ever.

*Maybe because I haven't found a man I wanted to take care of before.*

Me take care of Leo? Yes, I guess I'd like that. He deserves that.

"*Bella,* I'm so sorry it's taken me so long," Leo says, entering the room. He's lost his tie and a few buttons on his collared shirt are open as he rolls up his sleeves. I can't take my eyes off him. He's a man confident in himself and he commands the respect and attention in every room.

"You see something you like?" he says, laughing as he takes a glass out of the cabinet and pours some wine before joining me at the table.

I dig into my salad as Leo tells me about how Mateo caught him up on the latest situation.

"*Cara,* why didn't you tell me about Giorgio if what you heard upset you? I don't like you keeping things from me."

I put my fork down and turn my attention completely on him. "I wasn't keeping it from you, I promise. I trust you. I just wanted the chance to explain what I thought I heard in person, not through a text message. I felt crazy again when I say 'oh, I just had this bad feeling' and I wanted to read your expression. What do you think about the whole Giorgio thing? Him talking behind your back?"

He runs his fingers through his hair, clearly frustrated.

"I know that Giorgio can be very short-tempered. Italian businessmen all have that trait; I guess all Italian men in general," he says trying to reassure me. "But him talking behind my back doesn't matter —most people have something to say about their boss.

"What really upsets me is him talking to you about the shooter and implying that it's a man. I guess most people are quick to assume in terrible situations the criminal is a man, just look on the news—but that's not *always* the case. I have no idea who would want to shoot me; I can't list off a specific enemy. But like the police say, a high-powered person always in the spotlight can attract any kind of weirdo—even jealous or angry *women*."

"Do you think any of your ex-girlfriends would want to get back at you for anything?"

He lets out an exasperated breath. "We've spoken about this before, but of course you don't remember," he says, making me feel slightly embarrassed. "I don't have any ex-girlfriends. I took women on dates, but only a couple dates for each woman and then I'd move on. I was never with anyone seriously and I was never anyone's boyfriend— they all knew this and they were okay with the arrangements. But that doesn't mean that I didn't piss any of them off, though I hope not enough to want me dead."

*He's never had a girlfriend? Why me then?*

He said he's already spoken to me about this, and I'm going to guess I freaked out on him about it, like I want to right now.

*So remain calm and don't be annoying this time around. Act confident with yourself, damn it.*

"Okay enough of this super serious talk for tonight. Come with me," I say, taking Leo's hand and pulling us both out of our seats.

Leading the way with him still holding my hand, I take us up the stairs and into his bedroom. Opening the door, I step to the side to let Leo see what I spent my time doing while he was having serious boy talk with Mateo.

Vanilla candles sit on the dressers and rose petals lead the way to his four-poster king bed. I know these touches are super feminine and more to get me in the mood, but I have a few more tricks up my sleeve that will turn him on too.

*"Bella,* did you do this for me?"

"*Sì*, Mr. Beautiful. Now you're going to go sit your hot ass down on that bed, but not before I strip you out of these clothes," I say, reaching for the buttons on his shirt. I quickly throw it to the side and reach for his black belt, tossing that off too. I don't even think it takes 60 seconds to have all his clothes off and him standing in front of me in all his glory. He's smiling at me and I look down to see his cock is rock hard.

"Sit down," I command.

"Don't I get to undress you too?" he says, reaching for my T-shirt, but I grab his wrist, stopping him.

"I said sit down," I command again with a little more force in my voice as I push him back toward the bed.

I get out my iPhone and put on the sexy playlist I created just for tonight. Kelly Rowland's 'Motivation' plays as I begin a slow striptease to the music and fling my clothes toward him, trying to be as flirty as I can.

"Touch yourself," I whisper to him. He looks at me with a scowl and just when I think he's going to protest, he picks up his cock and strokes himself. Dear God, that's hot.

Taking my ponytail holder out, I toss my head as my hair falls around my shoulders in long waves.

I move my hips 'round and 'round—just like I learned when I took ballroom lessons back in college. As my hips move, I bring my hands up and down my own body, stopping to squeeze my breasts. Leo strokes himself slow and steady, matching my pace; he hasn't taken his eyes off me once. I can see he's fighting back taking control and commanding me to stop touching myself, but he doesn't. As the song ends, I'm completely naked and standing just out of arm's reach of Leo.

I open the top drawer of the nightstand and take out the things I brought with me.

A blindfold, sexy dice, and massage oil.

Leo eyes everything I've displayed on the bed. He releases his cock to grab my wrists and pulls me toward him. I fall on top of his bed and let out a moan as my wet sex rubs in just the right spot against his bulge.

He takes the black lace blindfold I was planning to use on him and puts it around my eyes, leaning me back to lay on the bed with my head on a pillow. It's quiet for a minute and my body is on high alert; I've never been blindfolded before. I can't believe I even bought these stupid toys! When I stopped by the lingerie shop again I noticed they had a little discrete corner filled with sex toys—I bought the tamest ones I could find.

"Get out of your own head," he whispers in my ear.

Heat radiates off his body as he hovers over mine. He sucks on my earlobe and trails kisses down my neck and collarbone heading toward my breasts. He stops and then after what feels like an eternity his hands are back on me.

He runs his hands, now slick with baby oil, down my chest and cups both of my breasts. He massages them and applies a little pressure; with the oil it feels divine.

His strong hands trail down my body slowly, bringing the oil down my stomach and over my hips. He spreads my legs open and slowly works his hands down my thighs. I arch my back a little and try to push my pussy toward his hands; I want him to touch me. He knows what I want and he's trying to tease me.

His hands are off me again and I hear him shift from the bed. It's quiet in the room and I swear I hear the door open and close.

*What the fuck? Did he leave me here? Is he walking around his house naked right now?*

I can't think of any more questions because I frantically jump when something ice cold lands on my stomach.

"Holy shit! Leo?" I ask to make sure a creeper hasn't just walked in the room. Hey you never know; I'm wearing a fucking blindfold.

"*Si bella*, it's me, don't worry," his says in his deep and raspy voice. His seductive tone tells me he's turned on.

The ice cube he placed on my stomach melts while he trails another piece around my right nipple before dragging it over to do the same on my left one. The sensation of the heat from the oil and the cold from the ice, plus not being able to see anything, makes my body hypersensitive. Leo trails another ice cube down from my tender breasts toward my stomach and then he hits the spot I've been waiting for. He puts the ice cube directly over my clit.

113

"Fuck," I hiss.

Reaching out to push the ice cube off me, he grabs my hands, stopping me from getting anywhere near my pussy. He interlocks our fingers, as I arch my back off the bed, still holding on to his hand.

"Don't fight it, Elena. Let the feeling take over," he says as he starts to circle the ice cube around my tight nub.

*I feel it alright! In every nerve in my entire body.*

The ice cube is flicked over and over my clit until its gone, replaced with Leo's warm mouth. Leo blows across my sex and the tingling I felt before is replaced with a new sensation.

Before I can get used to him blowing on me, he takes his tongue and runs it through my sex. I let go of his hand, needing to grip the sheet above my head. I'm ready to explode right this second.

He must know because he commands me, "Don't come yet, Elena. I will tell you when you can come."

Before I can argue, he returns his mouth to my sex and sucks. Leo takes what feels like two fingers and pushes them inside me. Between the ice and my excitement, I'm wet and waiting for anything he's willing to give me. He pumps his fingers slowly while continuing to suck and swirl his tongue.

"Fuck Leo, I can't wait much longer. Please ... please say I can come," I beg as I continue to grip the sheets for dear life.

If I let them go, then I'll let everything go. I'm right on the edge.

Then everything stops. His fingers are no longer inside me and his tongue is gone.

*What the fuck?*

"Leo, if this is you teasing me, I'm going to be really pissed off."

I hear him chuckle and then the bed shifts from his body weight. The blindfold is gently pulled off my head and it takes a second for my eyes to readjust to the room. Still dark and romantic, the candles are dimming and Mr. Beautiful is leaning next to me with a devilish smile.

It's cute and all, but this girl has needs and he has toyed with me long enough.

"Are you going to fuck me or not?" I spit out.

His smile quickly fades and he looks at me with hungry eyes. Those emerald eyes say it all—it's time.

Leo lies on top of me and positions his massive cock at my entrance and slowly, very slowly, pushes his way inside.

"Oh ... my ... god," is all I can manage to say as I tilt my head back in pure bliss.

He pushes a little more and I realize, holy shit, he's not even all the way in yet! *Is he going to break me?* No idiot, he's been inside you before! This isn't your real first time.

Leo must sense my mind is now running crazy with thoughts so he slams his cock the rest of the way inside of me as he also slams his mouth onto mine. His tongue swirls around my own at the same time he pumps his hips into me over and over. I try to push my hips up to meet his, but Leo's weight rests on me. I'm trapped beneath him and I love it. He cups the side of my face with his hand and continues to kiss me with such fierce passion.

"Elena, this is it," he growls with one final thrust hard into my pussy and, just like he commanded, I surrender to his control and my body gives into him. I feel his cock pulse inside and I squeeze my pelvic muscles together to give him a little thrill while he's coming down from his high still inside me.

His hand is still on my face and he collapses on top of me, this time letting me hold all his weight.

"Okay time for bed," he says, laughing.

"Get real lover boy, I don't think I can breathe."

He laughs even harder now and slowly pulls his cock from my sex, flopping next to me on the bed.

I let out a sigh, realizing I am truly spent. I don't think I've ever been as thoroughly fucked as I just was. I roll over to cuddle into his chest and I drift into the most blissful sleep ever.

———

Leo and I have been spending every night with each other. I hardly go to my apartment anymore except to restock the closet I'm slowly taking over at Leo's house. He hasn't mentioned me moving in with him, and I'm kind of worried that I'm overstepping my bounds. However, he must want me here because Mateo has orders to drive me here every night. I'm not going to ask him just in case it's too soon.

I haven't felt any uneasy feelings of being watched, but my routine is basic: work at the coffee shop, go to the gym, my apartment for some clothes, and then back to Leo's. We go out to dinners and we even took tango lessons one night, which was surprisingly lovely. I love dancing, but normally to a choreographed routine and without a partner. Leo is a great leader and, of course, being with a man who is confident is a turn on.

Leo spoke with Giorgio, but I'm still uneasy about the man. Giorgio chalked up his overheard outburst to having a bad day. He apologized and there haven't been any more outbursts; however, Leo has assured me there's a second set of eyes on his employee just in case.

Tonight Sophie and I are at the gym taking one of Alessandra's packed classes. I'm sweating out of every pore in my body. She's a great instructor and her students love her—including me! I haven't been such a great friend to Alessandra since the shooting and I feel bad about it. I got caught up in my own bullshit and the inner voices in my head trying to control me, when I should have let my friends in on my feelings instead of trying to figure it out myself. #ThatsWhatFriendsAreFor

After class the three of us head over to the juice bar across the street from the gym. I order a green juice and sit down at the outdoor patio. It's a gorgeous night, the sun is setting, and the temperature is cooling down a bit, unlike the hot and humid days. As much as I love every single minute spent with my man, there's something refreshing about being surrounded by girlfriends. And not just any girlfriends—girls who kick ass at all they do. I really hit the friend jackpot.

"So Sophie, tell us about your man?" Alessandra says, putting Soph in the hot seat. And get this ... Sophie actually blushes! It's the cutest thing ever to see my friend lose her cool over a man. And not just any man, someone as kind and loving as Marco.

"Girls, he's amazing!" Sophie squeals with excitement that's quickly matched by squeals from Alessandra and me! I think we are just as happy as Sophie.

"When I came to Italy, I told myself I would just take things slow because we haven't spent any time together face-to-face. I wasn't sure we'd like each other as much as we did over the Internet. But in person it's better! We click like we've been lifelong friends. It's crazy and kind of makes me nervous."

"Nervous how?" I ask.

"Nervous because I don't want to rush anything—but I feel so strongly for him already. We've spent so much time getting to know each other—and I feel dorky admitting this because I'm not one to go 'ga ga' over a dude," Sophie says taking a sip from her juice, "but I just want to keep everything perfect."

In unison Alessandra and I say "Awe!" toward Sophie.

"Okay, you girls are bitches. Enough about me. Tell me what's going on in your lives," Sophie asks.

We all launch into recaps. I tell them about my 'break' from Leo, which led to discovering I don't want that break at all, and I give them an update on the sadly bleak shooter situation.

Alessandra shares with us that she's walking her first runway show in Milan for the launch of a new fashion line that is supposed to be ridiculously amazing. I knew my friend was a rock star! Sophie and I tell her that we will be there and we couldn't be prouder. She also lets us know that she's dating—get this—a few men. She's definitely a fierce Italian woman who is a forced to be reckoned with.

After our juice bottles are empty and we can't stand the smell of our own stink—we didn't hit the showers after the gym because they were packed—we call it a night. I shoot Mateo a text letting him know we are done and he can pull the car closer. Mateo likes to give me space to feel like I'm not being watched, but it makes me happy to know he's right around the corner just in case I need him.

Alessandra, Sophie, and I double kiss our goodbyes and part ways.

Mateo still hasn't responded or pulled the car closer.

*What the heck?*

I send one more text just in case my first one didn't go through—but nothing. I see the car down the block and walk toward it. *Maybe he's in the bathroom?* I've never heard of Mateo taking a bathroom break, but I mean he's only human so he's got to! *Right?*

The back door is unlocked so I open it and climb in until I notice there's a body in the backseat.

A body is lying across the seat and upon closer look ... it's Mateo! *Oh my god!* My flight or fight response kicks in and I climb on top of him to check for his pulse—he's breathing! He has a large red bump across his temple and blood flows from a gash on his forehead.

Someone knocked him out and then put him here.

I stand back on the sidewalk and press the emergency number button on my iPhone. *Hurry up, hurry up!*

The operator speaks and before I can get a word out I feel a hard hit to my head and my body slams to the ground.

Then the world goes black.

# 16

---

"Okay bitch, it's time to open your eyes," I hear a man standing close to me shout.

My head is killing me and I don't want to open my eyes—everything hurts. I slowly pull my eyes open to see I'm in a dark room, a basement with small windows.

The muscles in my arms burn, but when I try to move I realize my arms are tied behind my back. I'm sitting on a wooden chair and I look down to see my legs tied together at the ankles. I'm trapped! #Panic

The familiar man's voice comes back into my focus, but I still can't see his face as his back is turned to me. He looks about average height and medium build wearing a black hoodie—nothing too threatening.

"Of course, you'd break your phone, you dumb slut."

*I broke my phone?*

A flash of memory returns quickly. I feel the pain again as I see in my mind's eye Mateo lying in the back of the car bleeding while I'm waiting to speak to the emergency operator before I was hit over the head. I fell to the ground and my face landed against my phone before hitting the sidewalk.

*Shit, how am I going to call for help now?*

That is if I weren't tied up—I can't call anyone; I can't even move.

"Why are you doing this?" I can barely even hear my own words as I whisper. My throat hurts badly, and I could really use a drink of water.

"Because you have what should have been mine! Both of you!"

And just then the man turns around ... Giorgio.

My heart drops down into my stomach and I feel like I'm going to throw up. I knew my instincts were right—this guy was bad news. He must also be the shooter; he knew he was a man all along because he is the shooter himself.

"Did you shoot me?" My voice is getting a little louder now, but it still hurts to talk.

*"Did you shoot me? Boo hoo."* he says in a mimicking voice.

"This doesn't make any sense. Were you aiming for me in the crowd? I thought the shooter was aiming for Leo?" My thoughts are spinning now, round and round, trying to remember anything from the shooting but still coming up blank. Damn it memories, now would be a great time to return.

Giorgio walks closer to me and I see the evil lurking behind his blue eyes. They don't look like the bright sky anymore, but pools of a deep dark ocean.

"I was aiming for Leo but you stepped in the way, causing a complication, like always, you dumb bitch."

Out of nowhere he slaps my face with full force. I spit out blood on impact. I also see drops of blood fall from my face to my yoga pants; I think my face must be cut from the glass of my phone and the rough ground.

"Why would you want to shoot Leo?" None of this is making any sense.

"I'm done answering your questions. Don't you see who the one in control is here?" For the first time I notice he's got a gun that he's now waving in front of my face. "Yeah ... it's me. So I ask the questions."

He walks out of my line of vision and I hear a door slam shut.

I'm alone now. Good, I can collect my thoughts. *How am I going to get out of here? Is Leo safe? Will Mateo be okay?* So many questions, but I silence them all. I need to focus and not lose my cool. I remember a meditation practice I learned in college and try to focus on only my breathing. My breath sounds loud in this quiet room. Besides this chair I'm tied to, I don't see anything else.

Giorgio leaves me here for what feels like hours, but I'm not really sure. I keep going in and out of consciousness. My head pounds, my muscles feel cramped in my entire body, and the ropes around my hands cut into my skin. I don't even know how much blood I've lost from my head. I'm dizzy and weak.

*This is it; this is how you will die.*

My heart clenches at the thought of not seeing Leo's face ever again and a single tear escapes my eyes.

I hear the door open from behind me.

"Crying like the big baby that you are? I knew it was a matter of time before you broke. Before I shoot you in the head, I do need some information from you," Giorgio says before squatting down in front of me. "I planned to use your phone to take the information from you and Leo that I need, but you ruined that. Of course, this makes the situation more problematic for me. So now I'm going to need you to play nice and answer a few questions."

Lifting my heavy head, I lock eyes with him. Then I do something I've never done before ... I spit on him. My bloody spit lands right on his face, and he looks shocked.

"I'm not telling you anything, you prick!" I shout.

"You cunt!" He stands up and then kicks me right in the chest with such strength that my chair is knocked back to the ground.

I land right on top of my tied hands and scream out in pain when I hear a loud crunch. I feel like my wrist just snapped.

"I'm going to leave you down there—on the ground just like a dog. You're going to think about what you just did bitch. And when I come back you will give me the answers I'm looking for."

And with that he delivers another swift kick right to my stomach before leaving the room.

This time he doesn't leave me alone for as long as before. He's growing anxious—he's pacing the room and mumbling under his breath now. I can't make out what he's saying because the pain in my head has grown—now including my ears. They ring and ring and ring.

Giorgio walks over to where I'm sprawled out on the floor and picks up the chair. He grabs my face between his sweaty hands and forces me to look at him. With him this close I can smell alcohol on his breath.

*Great, he's armed and drunk.*

He flashes his white teeth at me in an eerie smile and then he drops my face, which falls forward. I'm struggling to even hold my own head up. I hope this is over soon.

He gets my attention quickly though—when he shows me a new weapon, this time a knife.

"For every question you don't answer, I'm going to cut off one of your fingers," he says before placing the cold steel of the knife against my throat. "*Capisci?*"

I don't make a sound; no words come out.

"Do not make me repeat myself!! I said do you understand?" He shouts moving away toward a laptop propped on a small table.

I nod my head 'yes'—that's the best I can do right now. I'm fond of all of my fingers.

"I need to know the bank account information for not only your personal account but your business ones. I see your friend Sophie knows how to keep hackers at bay from your account information. That dumb cunt is lucky I didn't grab her tonight too."

*Sophie! I never realized that my friends could be in danger too!*

He must see the panic in my eyes; he knows he's got me right where he wants me.

"That's right, I have been following you for a long time. I waited patiently for you and those other two hens to stop gossiping before I made my move. Mateo proved to be a good opponent—until tonight. I realized that I'd have to sneak up on him to get him out of my way. He's always on alert, that *bastardo.*"

He's been waiting to make his move. Mateo was probably right when he spotted someone near my apartment, and I don't think I was crazy when I felt someone watching me in the piazza.

"I still don't understand why you are doing any of this. It can't just be about money. You have a good job, you are respected, you make money. Why are you doing this?" I plead for an answer. If I'm going to die tonight, then I want to know what the hell for.

"You want to know why I'm doing this?" He charges toward me, waving the knife in the air.

He's so close to my face that I lean back in the chair to separate us as much as I can.

"Yes," I whisper.

"I'm sick of having to compete with people who are entitled to everything they could possibly imagine. You know what it's like to work for someone who is younger than you but has the entire world at his fingertips? No, you don't, because you show up in his life, he has no idea who you are but he's landed himself a millionaire—a little American girl who has riches without having to face a single struggle. Both of you! People like you make me *sick*. Do you know what it's like to fight for your life? For your future? For fucking anything? I've had to work my way up and for what? *Niente.*"

No struggles? I can't speak for Leo, but I've had my fair share; however, I'm not about to argue with a man who has weapons.

"So if I give you all of my money will you let me go?"

And just like that, he laughs so hard that he has to hold his stomach as he folds over. He reminds me of the sneaky hyenas in *The Lion King* with their evil chuckle.

"Let you go? Are you crazy? So you can run to the cops to identify me as the shooter and now your kidnapper? Hell no! I will steal your money and Leo's money and then I will kill you and leave the country. Never to return to Italy again. I can go off somewhere else and build myself an empire and demand the respect that I deserve."

"You aren't going to get away with this," I say, not sure who I'm trying to convince—him or me.

"I might have the job title of marketing but I am one of the best hackers in the world. And I can disappear without a trace."

"So one of the best hackers in the world can't figure out how to break into a little American rich bitch's company account?"

*Oh great, now my sassy mouth decides to join the party!*

Let's blame it on the intense stress.

He slaps me with his free hand and then grabs my throat and chokes me. He's holding onto my neck tightly when he starts to lift me and the chair off the ground. All the oxygen is leaving my body when a loud bang startles both of us.

Giorgio drops me down, and luckily the chair remains upright, and he pulls out the gun he tucked in this waistband. He points it toward the door, and we hear another loud bang against it, and the next thing we know the door flies off.

Leo storms into the room and my heart is in instant panic. This man wants us both dead and now here we are in the same room together, making Giorgio's job that much easier. Giorgio looks just as shocked as I am to see Leo.

Leo only takes a second to look at me, and when he does his face transforms into a look of pure rage. I've never seen him appear this angry in all the time I've known him. And I must look like pure shit on the edge of life. I can see my pain reflected in Leo's eyes.

Just then he charges at Giorgio like he was a linebacker, throwing them both to the cement floor. Leo uses his own gun to knock Giorgio's out of his hands. Without a second thought, Leo pounds into Giorgio's face. Punch after punch, he does not let up.

"Leo, stop! You are going to kill him!" I hear myself screaming out. *Why not let Leo kill him? He sure as hell tried to kill us!* No, no I don't want to watch a man die and sure as hell don't want Leo to be a murderer.

Leo doesn't hear me or he's ignoring my shouts, as he continues to punch Giorgio in the face. Soaked in blood, Giorgio's face is completely unrecognizable and his breathing is very slow ... but he's still alive, just unconscious. His chest rises and falls.

Leo rushes over to me. He cups his hands around my face very carefully, but I still flinch at his touch.

"*Cara,* are you okay? I am so sorry this happened to you. The police are on their way," Leo reassures me.

"Leo, please untie me," I say while tears stream down my face. I'm officially in shock now.

Leo grabs the knife on the floor and starts to cut through the rope around my ankles and then runs behind my chair to cut the ropes around my wrists.

Before he gets the chance to finish with my wrists, Giorgio shouts at us, "You will pay for this!"

We let our guard down and Giorgio has gotten up off the floor. He's wobbly and his eyes look almost swollen shut, but he's definitely in control of his gun, which is pointed directly at us.

And then the rest of this scene unfolds around me in what feels like slow motion.

Giorgio fires his glock in my direction at the same time Leo throws my chair to the ground while he reaches for his own semi-automatic. Leo fires a shot at Giorgio and it's a direct hit. Giorgio grabs his chest and collapses to the ground. In an instant, he's in a pool of blood.

The last thing I see before blacking out is Giorgio take his last breath while lying on the floor, eye-to-eye with me.

# 17

**Leo**

I can't believe we are doing this again. I'm in a fucking hospital after yet another shooting waiting for Elena to gain consciousness. Déjà vu. I still hate hospitals and I hate the fact that since she's been in my life Elena has had to come here not once, but twice, all because of me.

Giorgio that fucking cocksucker.

I have known him for years. He was my intern when he was still in college and he worked hard during his internship that I immediately hired him after he graduated. He worked his way up in this company and not once did he act toward me in hatred. He never acted like having a younger boss bothered him.

I was thrown by the fact that Elena heard him talking shit about me, so I hired a private investigator to follow him around for a few days, but nothing came of it. Super boring—work, take out from restaurants, his home, repeat. I pulled the investigator off the case. I thought it was a waste of money.

Clearly, I fucked up.

But right now I'm so fucking grateful I didn't pull the tracker off

Giorgio's car. I knew when both Elena and Mateo were off the grid something was incredibly wrong, and I ran the tracking device.

Good thing I have a few friends on the police force who owe me a favor. They took my word that Elena was in danger and arrived at the abandoned farmhouse he was keeping her in shortly after I did.

When Elena was being taken to the hospital in an ambulance, I stuck around to speak with the police. I wanted to be by her side, but I needed to search this farmhouse to get some answers.

Together with the police, we searched through the whole place. If you saw it from the outside, then you'd think it was just another abandoned property on the outskirts of Rome, the windows boarded up and the grass overgrown.

Nothing to catch your eye.

The inside is pretty bare except for one bedroom that sets my nerves on edge. The police took pictures in that room, and it drew my attention, I had to see it for myself. When I walked in I was in shock. I'm so glad Elena was not there to see this. She'd lose her shit.

The bedroom walls are lined, floor to ceiling, with photos of Elena and me. Giorgio has been stalking me for what looks like the past year —with random women before Elena, and he's got photos of some very private moments between us as well. He has a laptop on a desk and the police are searching through the files after calling in one of their cyber security experts to get through all the passwords. I stand over the detective's shoulder trying to get a glimpse of anything I can.

Folders upon folders with my private information—he has everything you can imagine about me on this laptop. I bet he even knew my blood type. There's a folder on Elena as well. Pictures of our families, our employees, our degrees, our past lovers, private information on our companies, everything you can imagine.

Why does he want all of this?

An investigator walks over to me.

"*Signor* Forte, we are going to take this laptop into the station and we will let you know if we find anything that gives us a clue into why this man did this. Right now he looks like a classic stalker, with a real vengeance against you and your wife."

I don't correct him.

I want that to be the case more than anything, but if Elena doesn't want anything to do with me when this is all over, I wouldn't blame her.

## 1 8

**Elena**

Opening my eyes, I find myself yet again in a hospital, hooked up to more machines. Why does this keep happening to me?

Déjà freaking vu.

My entire body feels like I've been through hell and back. Even my eyelashes hurt, if that's even possible.

*Am I losing my mind?*

A nurse walks into the room and rushes to my bedside.

"Elena, how are you feeling?" She hands me a glass of water—I chug the whole glass, realizing how thirsty I really was. The nurse reads the stats from the machine I'm hooked up to and updates my medical chart.

"I'm going to get the doctor and I'll be right back."

She leaves me alone for just a second and then her and the doctor are back. I recognize him from the last time I was in the emergency room: Dr. Costa with his kind eyes and bushy mustache.

"Elena, we need to stop meeting like this," he jokes, smiling a wide smile.

"I hear you, doc! I'd rather we not meet at all if it's going to involve me in this bed hooked up to machines," I say, looking down at my arms and seeing bruises, deep cuts around my wrists, and a splint around my right arm from when I fell backwards in the chair.

"Elena, let me go through your list of injuries ... you've got a sprained right wrist, a concussion, cuts to your face, which we are treating for infection, and bruises all over your body—from your face to your feet. But, you are alive and your vital signs are good. It doesn't look like there's any internal damage."

I let out a huge breath. Each injury he listed brought back a memory of what Giorgio did to me.

*Giorgio, he's dead!*

*Leo, where's Leo?*

I must have asked my question aloud because Dr. Costa answers, "Leo's pacing the waiting room like a crazy man again. Driving the hospital staff up the wall with a million questions. We haven't told him that you were awake yet."

"Please get him, I need to see him."

"Of course. Anna, go get *Signor* Forte please," he says to the nurse, and she leaves the room in a hurry.

Leo storms into my hospital room and his eyes slowly take in my wrecked body—the splint around my arm, the bruises, the cuts—and it pains me to see how upset he is.

But when his gaze reaches my face all I can do is smile at him. I am happy. As crazy as that sounds—I'm really happy.

*Are these the drugs talking?*

No.

Okay, maybe a little.

I'm happy to be alive that's for sure. I'm happy that Leo is alive. I'm happy that we are in each other's lives.

"You saved me," I say, the first one to break our silence. Now he's the one to smile—it's a shy smile, like he's not really sure this is the appropriate occasion to be happy.

"Now we can call it even and call it quits."

"Quits ... on us?" I'm shocked.

"On us? Hell no, on this crazy 'saving each other's lives' game we keep playing. No more of this fucking bullshit," he says.

The nurse gives me a little more pain medication before leaving Leo and me alone.

His phone vibrates and I see a text message flash across his screen and the name of my best friend shows up.

"You know Sophie has been texting me non-stop. I told her and Marco I would give them updates and let them know when it was okay to show up. We kind of took over the hospital waiting room last time you were here," he says, typing a reply to my worried friends and family.

I'm grateful that he is the one taking care of all of this.

Leo laughs at his phone screen and then looks up at me.

"You know your friend is out of her damn mind. She wants to throw a party at my nightclub to celebrate you being alive."

Now this makes me laugh too! Sophie would see a reason to pop champagne at a time like this.

"You know what? She's right! We should have a celebration. Not just that I'm alive, but that you are too, and that we all are!"

"You are a remarkable woman, Elena Scott," Leo says. "So should I give Sophie the nightclub event planner's phone number? Should I warn her about Sophie first?" He laughs again.

Thinking about the nightclub makes me blush and Leo is quick to point it out.

"What has you blushing right now?"

"The nightclub ... that's where we—" My thought trails off to the memory of me leaning on that couch.

"Where we ... what?"

"You know... where you went down on me on that couch," I say, trying to avoid eye contact with him.

Leo looks at me like what I just said was the most important thing in the whole world. Like I just cured cancer or something.

"Uh, Leo—cat's got your tongue?" I tease.

"Elena, how did you know about what we did in the nightclub?"
*How did I know?*

"I remembered," I say, looking at him like #duh. Then it hits me. "Holy shit! I remembered!"

"What else do you remember?" he's quick to ask. He looks like a kid in a candy story—excited and eager for me to say something else.

"I remember ... everything, I think. I mean I have no clue what I don't remember," I say, laughing at how crazy I must sound. The drugs are starting to kick in for sure now. "I remember meeting you at the caffè, staring at your hot ass when you left, kissing in the cleaning supply closet, the nightclub, the pool, my trip to Milan with the girls, you wanting to be lovers and then surprising me at the charity ball when you told everyone I was your girlfriend. The charity ball." I sigh in between all the memories flashing back to me with the next one hard to relive. "I remember overhearing your mother and Victoria saying how I'd never be good enough for you. I thought they were right. It really hurt me that they couldn't accept me for who they thought I was—even though they had no clue."

Leo grabs my left hand and slowly brings it to his lip to place a delicate kiss upon it.

"Elena, why didn't you feel comfortable telling me who you really were? I understand not in the beginning, but at some point you could have."

I take a deep breath and confess.

"It's not that I wasn't comfortable. I'm not ashamed of all that I've accomplished or being a successful woman. What upset me at first was I didn't want any man to only want me because of all those things—which was the case back in America. I figured I'd come to Italy and not let anyone know. With you, I knew you wouldn't care about 'using me' for success because you have your own set of very impressive accomplishments—more than mine."

I take my hand back from his and twiddle my fingers—a nervous habit when I feel anxious. He doesn't say anything, giving me the time I need to compose my thoughts before starting again.

"With you ... I was crushed that all these people—who I assumed were very influential in your life—were very vocal about their hate for me. If these two women thought that, then what would the rest of the country think? Everyone watches every single thing that you do.

"And, if they don't like me for my personality or my character, which I was always true to from the beginning, then they don't deserve to know anything else about me. About the business side of me."

Leo looks down at me and composes his thoughts.

"Elena, what those women think doesn't mean anything to me. I don't need anyone's approval for anything I do in my life—and I've lived this way since I was a kid. I can normally be a good judge of a character—except for Giorgio." He looks down now at his hands. "But with you—you were different. From the beginning, I was initially attracted to you because of your beauty. But it was far more than that. When I caught you daydreaming at the counter in the coffee shop, I think from that moment I knew I had to know you better. And I'm glad you let me chase you—you are a kind, smart, beautiful, generous woman and I am proud to be with you. If anything, *I* am the one not good enough for *you*."

I let what he says sink in, afraid that if I speak, then something smart ass will come out and I will ruin this moment.

No one has ever said such lovely things to me before, and I know Leo—he doesn't bullshit when he speaks, he gives it to you straight. Good or bad. And this was ... too much.

Tears run down my face and before the drugs officially take over and I drift off to La La Land, I manage to say, "I love you."

———

I wake up from a drug-induced sleep—which was lovely and I realize I'm now in another hospital room. This one looks less scary because I'm no longer in a single room alone. There's a drape separating my hospital bed from another person in the room.

"Hello," I whisper.

Who knows who could be over there and in what condition? I would hate to wake someone up from a pleasant sleep. As pleasant as sleep can be inside a hospital.

"Elena," I hear a deep voice say back through the white sheet.

They know me? It's then I realize I'm a terrible friend because I

133

forgot one of the most important people to me was also hurt in this mess.

"Mateo!" I scream out.

I reach as far as I can outside of my bed to grab the drape with my good hand and I pull hard to get it to swing back. There he is lying in the bed beside me.

"I think you are taking this 'always on duty' thing I bit too far." He breaks out in a smile and we both laugh.

"How are you feeling?" I ask him—noticing he has a white bandage wrapped around his forehead, which I spot dried blood on.

"So much better now that I see you are okay. I'm so sorry for this, Elena," Mateo says in the most serious voice I've heard. And that's a lot coming from him.

"Mateo, are you out of your mind? This is in no way your fault. Giorgio was insane and he was going to get to Leo and I in any way he could—I'm just so upset that it had to involve hurting you. I was scared out of my mind when I found you in the car," I confess.

I haven't really talked about what happened to me in this whole ordeal. The police are coming back tonight for my statement—trying to give me time to recover.

"When I woke up in the back of an ambulance I was upset. Then when I found out you were missing I went to another level of pissed off. If Leo hadn't killed that man, I would have," Mateo says.

I realize just how lucky I am to have such protective men in my life looking out for me.

"Mateo, you are truly a great man," I say trying to pass my smile along to his grave face, "And I hope your boss gives you an awesome vacation after all of this! You deserve it!"

We both laugh until a nurse walks in to see what all the commotion is about. I guess laughing uncontrollably isn't a normal reaction from trauma patients.

# 19

## One Month Later

The police just left Leo's home after an intense briefing on the shooting-turned-kidnapping and assault-turned-death.

What an experience. If it hadn't happened to me, I would have thought it was a movie.

The police searched the abandoned farmhouse, which legally belonged to Giorgio, and other than the room Leo found with the police, it was completely empty. I'm glad I wasn't there to see it; I would have had nightmares for the rest of my life.

Instead, I did see police photos of the crime scene. Giorgio had the entire room covered in photos of us and even more on his computer.

But it looked like the obsession started before me. Giorgio wanted Leo's life and everything in it. The police say he acted out of pure jealousy and rage. Some stalkers take things to the next level. I believe they say he falls into the 'Resentful Stalker' category. Police also investigated Giorgio's apartment and found that he was collecting Leo's trash.

I'm sad that Giorgio had to die—he could have sought some kind of help—but with him attacking me, the police say there was no hope.

Someone would have been carried out of that basement in a body bag— and I'm grateful it was not Leo or me.

Leo did not face any charges for killing Giorgio because he acted out of self-defense. I don't think he was ever worried about charges; he was acting on his instinct to keep me safe, and I know he would do anything for me, as I would for him. We've both proven that to each other and I don't think we need to do any more of that again.

I'm still in a splint but I should be able to take it off soon. The bruises and cuts are healing nicely. Most of them are gone now, a few still slightly yellow where I was punched in the face.

"*Bella,* you ready to go to dinner?" Leo says, coming into the room with a towel wrapped around his waist and a few drops of water on his chest. #Drool

"Do we really need to go? I'd rather you ditch the towel and get over here." I lick my lips and wink at him.

He laughs at my bad attempt to seduce him.

"I would love to drop this towel and bury myself deep into your tight pussy. But *you* are the one who set this dinner up, and I think even if we skipped, Sophie would somehow make her way over here to hang out with you. So if you don't want them to catch us naked, we should go."

"Why do you always have to be right?"

I head toward the walk-in closet in Leo's bedroom that I've officially taken over. It's a good thing he has two. I've stayed here every single night since I left the hospital, and I don't miss my apartment or having my private space at all. I like sharing my time and my space with Leo.

However, he has yet to say anything about me giving up the apartment to live here with him permanently. Actually we haven't even spoken about when I'll go back to Michigan. I have to go back at some point, right? I mean my company is there.

*Who am I trying to convince here?*

*Yourself, stupid.*

I'm deep in thought that I don't even realize that Leo has walked into my closet until he touches me, scaring the crap out of me! He was trying to brush my long hair aside to help me zip up my tight black dress.

"You okay, *bella?*"

"Yep," I manage to squeak out before stepping into my stilettos. The mood feels different now as I think of moving back to Michigan and being far away from the one person who forces my heart to beat.

*Forces my heart to beat?*

When did I become this sappy love-struck girl? Damn Leo, he's got me good.

I don't want to leave him. I just don't wanna. #Pout

———

The waiting list of this restaurant is miles long, but Mr. Beautiful knows the right people and our reservations were immediately made.

"Well, don't you two just look like the hottest couple Rome has ever seen," Sophie says as we approach the table where she and Marco are waiting for us.

"I could say the same thing back to you two," I say, taking my seat next to the window.

I can't help but to marvel at the view. This is the city I've grown to cherish, and I'm sitting here with the man I'm madly in love with and two of my closest friends. What a perfect night this would be if my head weren't in clouds of worry.

"I hope you don't mind we ordered a bottle for the table and Caprese appetizers," Marco says, before dipping a piece of fresh bread into a dish of olive oil.

Italian bread—it's to die for! I join him and take a slice for myself before Sophie fills us in on all the fun things she and Marco have been doing around Rome. Watching her excitement as she talks about all the fun they are having together makes me ecstatic to be able to help her out. She asked me if she could work from Italy while she's here—of course I said yes—but in a week she'll be headed back to Michigan.

Michigan—the topic I want to avoid but can't seem to escape tonight.

"Elena! Snap out of it girl," Sophie says, nudging my arm. I see the three of them staring at me. Of course, I was off in my own world.

"Sorry! My mind has been all over the place lately," I say.

"How did everything go with the police today?" Marco asks.

Leo fills them in on what the police told us, but I feel Sophie's eyes trying to make contact with mine. I'm refusing to look over at her. I know, I'm so mature. She'll be able to read right through me if I look at her, and I don't want her to see that it's not what the police had to say that's got my mind so scattered.

"Excuse us, we are going to use the ladies room," Sophie says as she grabs my hand and pulls me from the table.

"I didn't know I had to use the bathroom?" I say to my best friend, but with her death grip on my hand I have no choice. We are going to the bathroom.

"Women can't help but travel in packs to the bathroom," Marco says to Leo, and they both laugh.

We walk to the posh bathroom, with dark marble counter tops that complement gold wall mounted faucet sets—this place is so fancy I'm surprised there's not a lady inside handing out towels.

Sophie grabs me by the shoulders and looks me straight in the eyes.

"Okay spill it. What has you so upset? It's not the stalker situation, I can tell. I want the truth."

"I'm going to have to go back to Michigan."

"Well ... duh. When are you thinking of going back?"

"That's the thing, I haven't thought about it at all. It just hit me before we came here that at some point I have to return. My company is there, my family is there, my apartment, my ... everything."

"Not your man."

"And that's the reason I'm upset. Why am I living this fairy tale now if I have to leave it at some point? Leo's whole life is here. He won't follow me."

"Girl, listen, you run a social media marketing firm. What do we always teach our clients? Social media allows them to run their businesses from anywhere with the Internet. The world is at their fingertips! And it's at yours too, Elena. And ... if you so happen to want to setup an office here in Italy, I might know at least one of your employees who would help you," she says with a wink.

*An office here in Italy?*

She's right, social media happens anywhere. It's the freakin' Internet.

Duh. Why didn't I think of that?

And the rest of the stuff? Well my apartment I can sell, and my parents can come visit me or I'll go visit them. My family would never want me to turn down love. The heavy dumbbell crushing my heart has been lifted. Now I just need to get Leo to ask me to stay. I mean, I sure as hell am not going to force myself onto him if he doesn't want me. I don't want to look desperate.

"Sophie, you are a genius!" I squeal with excitement as I embrace her in a hug and kiss her cheek.

"Well, I already knew that, but it's nice having someone say it. Now let's stop this ridiculously cute love fest and go back to our hunky Italian men. Who knew I'd be saying that sentence one day? " she says, still locked in my tight embrace.

———

Our dinner was delicious and it's nice to double date with Sophie. We've never done this before. We've both had our fair share of boyfriends in the past, and when we weren't with crazies—well, mine were almost always crazy—us girls were so focused on our careers that we didn't go out much.

Neither of us mentioned our conversation in the bathroom when we came back to the table, but I could tell the guys knew something happened in there. I came back to the table in a great mood—gone was my super sour attitude from before.

On the car ride back to Leo's we kept the conversation light and held hands the entire way. I almost worked up the nerve to say something about if I should call this place home for me too, but I chickened out.

I'm now curling up on the couch in a grey fleece blanket staring into a mesmerizing fire with a cup of French Vanilla flavored coffee in my hand. I wanted to continue with the wine, but my Mr. Beautiful was set on after dinner coffees.

He was so adorable about it, I didn't argue.

Leo popped out of the room to take a phone call from Mateo, but he promised it would be quick. He also promised me something not-so-quick when he returns: his cock buried deep inside me.

His dirty words, not mine, even though I love saying them.

Being with Leo sexually is unlike anything I've ever experienced. And I'm not just talking about the mind-blowing sex. Yes, that's in a class of its own, but I'm talking about how I feel before, after, and during it. Like a new woman.

Someone confident in herself, not just in a boardroom, but also in the bedroom. I want him to look at me and devour my entire body with his eyes, I want him to touch me with fingertips that light my skin on fire, I want to make him growl my name while I pleasure him.

Gone is the timid woman in the bedroom who made sure the lights were off and worried about sucking in her stomach while doing it doggy style, which was just about the only position my past boyfriends wanted. So creative. Not with Leo—I want it all, everything he can give me. And I want to give him all of me in return.

"You must be thinking about something good," Leo says as he joins me on the couch with his own cup of coffee.

"Why do you say that?"

He always catches me when I'm daydreaming.

"You had a huge smile on your face just now. I almost didn't want to interrupt you," he says, as he trails his fingers up and down my arm. "But putting off making love to you is not something I am willing to do."

"Making love? I don't think I've heard you call it that before. Always 'fucking' or something equally dirty." I joke with him but my heart skips a beat at the idea of us 'making love' to one another.

"*Cara*, I might speak dirty but everything I feel for you is pure love."

"You are definitely a different guy than the one in his office who was trying to convince me to be your *lover*." I say the word with a mocking tone, but he can tell by my wide smile that I'm just kidding.

"*Sì*, lovers. You hated that word and everything it stood for. I don't blame you at all. You are worth more than that. Much more. I was a stubborn Italian man back then, set in his ways. I'm glad you came along to change them. Now hurry up and finish that coffee."

"Bossy aren't we?" I laugh.

He must want to get right down to the nitty-gritty. And I don't blame him! I'm equally eager to get Mr. Beautiful naked, have some crazy passionate lovemaking, and then try to get him to bring up the idea of me moving to Italy for good.

Taking my last sip of coffee, I notice something at the bottom of the cup I've never seen before. It looks like there are too many coffee grounds, but then I see there's a message: the words '*Marry Me*' are printed in black on the inside of the white cup.

My heart stops and my breath hitches.

While I am studying my cup as if the words are going to disappear at any moment, I don't even realize Leo is off the couch and kneeling down in front of me.

*Holy shit! He's kneeling!*

"Elena, you are a stubborn woman," he says as he takes my hand and I laugh, "but you are *my* stubborn woman. You fought hard against the idea of being just my *lover* and I'm glad you did. You have been different from the start. From the time you accidentally asked me what you could '*do to me*' in the coffee shop to the moment you saved my life —and all the craziness in between—I wouldn't take them back for anything.

"I knew after the shooting that I wanted to do this. When I thought that you could possibly not be in my life every single day, I drove myself insane. I knew that I did not want that day to come, and I also realized how much I absolutely love you. *Ti amo, solo tua*," Leo says as he reaches into his pocket and pulls out a ring box. "Elena Scott, will you marry me?"

*Marry him! I think I'm going to throw up my coffee.*

Putting my cup down on the coffee table, the next I know, I'm tackling him to the ground. I'm lying on top Leo, kissing him with all my force. Electricity sparks through my body, and I feel like I'm floating on cloud nine. Someone pinch me.

It's like he read my mind. Leo spanks my ass and I know I'm not dreaming. I'm tingling from head to toe. Leo pulls at my dress as I help him get it over my head. I'm not wearing a bra and his hands instantly dart to my breasts, cupping each one. He rolls his thumbs around each nipple and I arch back with a little moan.

Ever so slowly he takes his sensuous mouth and sucks on each breast. I can't take it much more. I'm so wet for him and I want him to know. Grabbing the bottom of his shirt, I pull it over his head, revealing his strong muscles.

Pushing him back down, I run my hands along his chest. I plant kisses down his chest until I get to that sexy 'V' waiting for me at his hips. I unzip his pants and slide them off along with his boxer briefs. I take a second to ditch my undies.

We are both completely naked and glorious! I massage his massive thighs, slowly bringing my hands closer and closer to his cock. I see evidence that this is turning him on too.

Neither of us has yet to say a word. This moment does not need any words. I bring my entrance to his cock and grind on top of him. Swiveling my hips, I hold my hands to his chest while I let my body take over as I ride my man. My clit finds just the right spot to rub on his cock, and I buck my hips a little more.

Before I can scream out, Leo flips us over and now he's on top of me. He locks eyes with mine and then thrusts his manhood inside of me.

*Harder! Faster! Please!*

It's like he reads my mind again. Leo knows just what I need, thrusting harder and faster into me. I dig my nails into his back to hold on. He pumps into me with such passion I can't hold out any longer—we orgasm together in what feels like an explosion of my senses.

With his cock still inside me, Leo pushes my hair to the side and whispers into my ear, "I take that as a yes, *bella.*"

I laugh and then cup his face between my hands and stare into those emerald eyes that caught my attention when we first met.

"Yes, yes, yes! I can't think of anything I want more in this entire world than to be your wife," I say before claiming his mouth again in a soft yet passionate kiss. "Now let me see that ring!"

"You'll get a glimpse of it after one more round. Keep up *Signora* Forte."

And with that he takes me again and again. I couldn't be happier. I smile to myself thinking about that ridiculous wish I made at the Trevi Fountain not once but twice. It's just come true.

My happily ever after.

The End—*Fine*

From the bottom of my heart, THANK YOU for reading The Eternal City Love series.

It would mean the world to me if you left a review on Amazon. <3

**Fun update!** Leo and Elena make a special guest appearance in my latest novel, Encounters In Disguise, which is book 2 in The Signs Series.

For updates on how their lives have been in Italy for the last few years, you'll want to check that out. It's also in Kindle Unlimited.

## CATERINA WANTS TO HEAR FROM YOU

To visit Caterina's website and join her newsletter list, head to:
http://www.caterinapassarellibooks.com

### STAY SOCIAL
Find Caterina on her Facebook page at:
http://www.facebook.com/catpassarelli

Instagram:
http://www.instagram.com/caterinapassarelli

TikTok:
http://www.tiktok.com/@caterinapassarelli

# ACKNOWLEDGMENTS

## With Love

Thank you to my parents & siblings for always believing in me— no matter what crazy idea I come up with! Your support, guidance, and unconditional love mean the world to me. Now only read this section of the book! ;)

To my best friends who encouraged me to write my dirty novels, let me discuss the world of book publishing with them, cheered me on and celebrated with me. You know who you are.

To Team Movement, without the support of my fun loving fitness family I would never have the guts to go after any dream. And to Beachbody, who if I never partnered with to be a coach I would not be able to have the freedom to spend time writing.

To the people who helped me get the Eternal City Love series ready for publication. Najla Qamber for designing the breathtaking covers & Duncan Koerber for editing and brainstorming with me.

To the readers, without you Leo and Elena's story would be just my own. Now we get to share it together.

## ALSO BY CATERINA PASSARELLI

The Eternal City Love Duet

My Mr. Beautiful

Fighting For Mr. Beautiful

The Signs Series

Fortunate Encounters

Encounters In Disguise

^Leo and Elena also show up in this novel

Contemporary Standalones

The Power of Salvation

Thirty Dates Later